Revenge by Fire

BILL WILLIAMS

A Black Horse Western

ROBERT HALE · LONDON

ISBN 978-0-7090-8821-9

Robert Hale Limited
Clerkenwell House
Clerkenwell Green
London EC1R 0HT

www.halebooks.com

Typeset by
Derek Doyle & Associates, Shaw Heath
Printed and bound in Great Britain by
CPI Antony Rowe, Chippenham and Eastbourne

ONE

'Where shall we bury them, Mr Shelton?' Ed Foley asked.

Conrad Shelton turned to his foreman seated on the grey mare alongside him and gave him a long hard look, indicating that he'd spoken out of turn. Some of the men in the lynching party had started to unfasten the shovels tied to their saddles. They were all eager to get the hell out of the secluded clearing where more than a few men had drawn their last gasping breath. The sky had gone dark and there had been a distant roll of thunder. It had seemed as though the welcome rain would come and end the drought, but now the sky had turned blue again, except for the odd white cloud.

Ed Foley shifted uneasily in his saddle waiting for his instructions. He'd experienced Conrad Shelton's ruthlessness during the many years he'd worked for him, but he wasn't prepared for what was coming.

Conrad Shelton puffed on the fat cigar as he pondered on the question. He was sixty-five years old and had steely grey hair. His once powerful frame had long since turned to fat through rich living. The heavily jowled face was more flushed than usual.

'You can bury their heads, but leave the rest where they're hanging. Make sure you strip them naked, so it will make it easier for the vultures and don't forget to brand them. When you're done here you can all celebrate in the saloon. I think the town should give you men a hero's welcome for catching those three. Oh, and Foley, give the men ten dollars each and tell the barman at the Elm House saloon that I'll be paying for the drinks.'

Conrad Shelton turned his magnificent white stallion away from the group and urged it forward into a gallop. Now his grandson, Daniel wouldn't have to leave the family home and need have no fear for his life. Those excuses for human beings had sent their last threatening message!

'You heard what the boss said,' Foley barked, intending Shelton to hear him, but the wealthy ranch owner was already out of earshot.

'Hadn't we better wait for them to die?' asked Tim Aitkin, whose face still hadn't lost the paleness it had taken on since he'd heard the gruesome instructions.

'What!' Foley snapped at the youngest member of the group. 'They all look pretty dead to me and if they're not then we'll hear them squeal when we brand them, won't we?'

Aitkin didn't intend arguing with the fiery foreman, but he'd seen one of the men open his eyes as Conrad Shelton had ridden off. Tim Aitkin was only seventeen years old, a gawky, slightly built lad and he'd puked the first time he'd seen his pa wring the neck of a chicken. He knew that his face must be as pale as a ghost, but at least he hadn't peed in his pants.

'Are we really going to do like the boss said?' queried Jim Tully, one of the senior members of the gathering and the only man who would dare ask such a question.

'You bet,' Foley replied. 'You've been around long enough, Tully, to know that you do what Conrad Shelton orders, unless you don't mind leaving this part of Arizona, because he'd make certain you would never find work here for as long as he lives.'

Tim Aitkin was reluctant to say what was puzzling him, but he eventually mustered up enough courage and asked in a timid voice that hadn't been broken long, 'Mr Foley, if those men are headless, won't the rope slip? I don't see how a man can hang if he hasn't got a head.'

Ed Foley glowered at Aitkin before he shook his head, then he smiled and replied, 'You've got a good point there, kid. You're not as daft as you look.' He addressed the other men, 'Why didn't one of you dumb asses think of that?'

Foley was forty-two years old, heavily built with greying hair and dark brown eyes. Some of the men were as frightened of him as they were of Conrad Shelton and he had a reputation for solving any problems with his fists. But he could have a soft spot when he was in the mood.

Foley ordered some of the men to pull down the dangling figures and drag them towards the fire where the branding iron was glowing red. Even the horses seemed spooked by what was taking place. Foley only applied a light touch of the iron to the backs of each man, but Tim Aitkin was soon struggling to keep his breakfast down when the smell of burning flesh reached his nostrils. The wetness inside his trousers told him that he'd lost the battle. He just hoped that the trickle didn't reach his boots.

Only Foley knew the real reason why these three men had been dragged from their small log cabin and subjected to a beating before having a noose tightened around their necks. Foley had said that they had been warned about cattle rustling, but no one could recall when this was supposed to have happened. It wasn't as though the men had any land that Shelton might have wanted to acquire, which was his usual motive for terrorizing people until he got his own way. It just didn't make sense, but Shelton's men always did what they were told.

Tim Aitkin wasn't the only man in the group who'd been relieved when Foley had made the surprising announcement that he would take care of the beheading himself. He told them that they could leave for town once they had stripped the men's clothes off and secured a rope underneath their arms so that they wouldn't fall to the ground after the beheading. He instructed the men to leave the wagon behind because he intended to stand on it while he carried out Shelton's instructions to sever the heads.

Tim Aitkin was the last in the group as they rode off and when he looked behind he could see Ed Foley take his large hunting knife from its sheath. It made Aitkin wince at the thought of what it was about to be used for.

The men had soon whipped their mounts into a full gallop, eager to get away from the carnage in which they had taken a part. The images would not leave them easily, but they would soon be dulling their memories, at least for a short while by drinking hard liquor paid for by Conrad Shelton who was on his way home to hear some unexpected and shocking news.

TWO

Marshal Ron Waters sighed and his face took on a worried look as he walked towards the Elm House which was Craigy Plains's only saloon and whorehouse. The cause of his anxiety was the rider he'd watched ride down Main Street and tie the reins of his dapple grey horse to the hitch rail outside the saloon.

'That's all I need,' the marshal muttered to himself. He hadn't been looking forward to tonight because he expected the usual bunch of Shelton's men to come into town and now there was a prospect of more trouble. He had been Marshal of Craigy Plains for close to eight years and the job hadn't got any easier. Marshal Waters had been a stocky, powerfully built man, but a recent illness had caused him to lose some weight and he'd also lost some of his old energy. His black hair was still thick, but was grey at the edges. The brown eyes had been dulled by a series of tragic events, including the recent loss of his only son who had died in an accident at his army barracks in Wilcox Creek. His wife Anne had left him five years ago when he'd refused to hand in his badge after he'd been gunned down during a bank robbery. She'd just got fed up waiting to be made a widow.

The marshal had a special affection for the town which had seen many changes and, like most towns in Arizona, had thrived since the introduction of the railroad. The stagecoach still stopped there twice a week, but the lifeblood of the town was the large Shelton ranch that provided work for so many and was the main reason for the town's prosperity. The smaller ranches didn't derive the benefit that the Shelton ranch enjoyed from the water provided by the nearby river, and all of them were in danger of going out of business because of the drought.

'Let's have no brawling tonight, Ross,' the marshal shouted out as he made his way towards the man who had caused him grief so many times.

'Evening, Marshal,' Steve Ross replied with a smile. Ross was twenty-five years old and tall with broad shoulders. Considering that he rarely left a saloon without his knuckles being grazed and bloodied, his square-jawed face was unmarked except for the thin crease across a nose that had been broken only once. His smiling eyes and his easy-going manner had fooled many a man into thinking that Ross was nothing special. Even some who had known what he was capable of had made the mistake of thinking that they would beat him in a fight and enhance their own reputation.

Ross liked the marshal, mainly because he was fair, but he wished the old-timer would hand in his badge and go fishing, or do some relaxing. He'd slowed down this past year and the town had more than its share of troublemakers.

Ross smiled again and gave the marshal a promise, 'I'll do my best, Marshal and, as always, you have my word that I won't be the one to start anything, but I do aim to have more than just a few beers. I've been working on that dustbowl of mine all week, but I don't know why I bothered.'

The marshal expressed his sympathy and told him that he'd seen one of Ross's neighbours earlier when he'd called into town to get some supplies before he moved on, and he wasn't the first. Some men had put their heart and soul into building up their farms, hoping that it would be a legacy for their children, but had been forced to give in to nature. Some good men had turned to a life of crime in order to survive and only the most determined and stubborn remained.

'Actually, Marshal, I've got some good news for you because this will be my last night in town, at least for a while. I'm moving on myself tomorrow,' replied Ross.

The marshal had some news that he decided to pass on to Ross.

'Well, that's a shame, Ross. I was talking to Red Ron Sherrington at the railroad office yesterday and he told me that one of the engine drivers reported seeing some light rain falling north of the Craigy Mountains. Red Ron has written a poem about the drought and he insisted on reading it to me. I suppose his poetry writing helps him to pass the time. He usually writes about the Indians, which in case you don't know is how he got his name when he was working as an Indian interpreter for the cavalry.'

'If the heavens open tonight I'm still moving on tomorrow,' Ross quipped, then mounted the steps to the sidewalk and pushed open the swing doors of the saloon, leaving the marshal with a disappointed look on his face.

Dooley, the barman carried on mopping the beer slops

11

from the bar, but his face had a concerned look to match the marshal's when he spotted Ross.

'Here comes trouble,' muttered Dooley under his breath as he reached for a glass.

'What'll it be, Steve? Are you feeling thirsty, or do you want some fire in your belly?' Dooley liked Steve, even though his visits to the saloon usually meant extra work clearing up the broken glass and tidying up the scattered tables and stools.

'Ross always lights my fire,' said Lisa, who managed the saloon girls, as she sidled up and sat on a stool next to where Ross was standing.

No one knew Lisa's exact age, but most would have guessed it was the high side of forty. The blonde hair rested on her shoulders and there was no doubting that she had been a pretty woman, but now the make-up was thick to hide the wrinkles around the mouth and eyes. The breasts were no longer firm, but the figure still looked good and tempting to most drunken cowboys.

'Make it a beer, Dooley, and keep them coming,' replied Ross after he had pondered whether he wanted to start with a whiskey. He turned to Lisa and smiled.

'No, I'm not going to buy you a drink, Lisa, at least not now. But if you come back later I might have softened up a bit. Then maybe I'll treat you, but I think by then I'll have run out of money. Times are hard for us farming boys.'

Lisa looked disappointed and eased herself off the stool. 'Don't leave it too late, because I might have settled in upstairs with some lucky cowboy. By the way, my two new girls, Lily and Kathy, were quizzing me about you last night and before you ask, Marielou will be singing tonight now

12

that her throat is better. She thinks it's all the smoke from that strong baccy that some of the boys smoke. That girl worries me sometimes, and I keep telling her that she needs to get a man who will bring a bit of colour to her lovely face.' Lisa winked at Ross and walked away, wriggling her butt in that provocative way that she always did, knowing that she was being watched.

Ross was pleased that Marielou would be singing again because she had the voice of an angel and she was pleasing on the eye. He couldn't quite figure out why she'd ended up in a place like the Elm House, because she wasn't like the other girls, who were out for a good time and making money. In some ways she reminded him of Stephanie Shelton. The thought of Stephanie had him reaching for his beer. He intended to enjoy tonight and he didn't want any melancholy thoughts to spoil it.

Ross had just taken his first gulp from his second glass of beer when he heard the noisy entrance of the two men as they made their way to the bar.

'Two whiskeys, ugly,' shouted the taller one before ordering his buddy to pay for them. Dooley wasn't exactly God's gift to women and he was a little on the weedy side, but he wasn't what many folk would describe as ugly, except for the slight hook in his nose. Dooley gave the newcomers a weak smile and tried to make polite conversation with them before he was cut short with another insult.

'Just do like Deak says and pour the drinks,' said the chubby-faced stranger, who had a mixture of yellow and green teeth, then he added, 'I reckon your pa and ma must have worked in the circus and been in one of those freak shows.' The two men laughed and Dooley's latest tormentor turned away to survey the saloon as though he was weighing up any likely opposition. He gave a snigger to go with his disapproving look towards those who looked in his direction. The men who looked his way mostly quickly averted their eyes, but Ross wasn't one of them and held eye contact with the troublemaker until he turned away from Ross.

'There doesn't look like much action in here, Morrie. This town is about the biggest shithole I've ever seen this side of the Craigy Mountains, and it smells funny as well. Judging by that old hag over there we won't be seeing what upstairs is like either, but I might go with her if she pays me, although I reckon my horse is prettier than she is.'

The men laughed again as Lisa made her way towards them, taking a long drag on her cigarette as she moved. There was no wiggle in her walk this time and her face was set in an expression that would have frightened some cowboys. She stopped in front of them and slowly looked Deak up and down, as though she had been asked to guess what size trousers he wore. He looked uncomfortable even before she said, 'I bet your mouth is the only big thing you've got, mister.' Lisa drew hard on her cigarette, then blew smoke into his face.

A group of cowboys sitting at a card-table near the bar laughed at Lisa's remarks. One of them said. 'Why, have you seen it, Lisa?'

The card-players all laughed again. Deak glowered at Lisa and then at the men who had found her remarks so funny. It seemed for a moment that he was trying to find the right words for a reply, but he failed and slapped her hard across the face, causing her to fall against the bar.

Then he shouted into her face, 'You painted bitch.'

Lisa ran her hand across her face and felt the warm blood on her fingers and the throbbing from her lips. She put her hands in front of her face as Deak raised his arm ready to strike her again. She waited for the blow, but it never came. She cried out when she heard the thump, thinking he had struck her again, but Ross had delivered a heavy punch to the side of Deak's face, sending him crashing to the floor.

Morrie was too slow in reaching for his pistol and Ross delivered a vicious blow to his nose that caused a spurt of blood and sent Morrie sprawling on top of the fallen Deak. Deak pushed Morrie to one side and struggled to his feet. He tried to throw a punch at Ross, who blocked it with his arm and delivered a vicious blow to Deak's jaw. The sound of bone on bone was followed by a loud thud as Deak fell backwards, hitting his head on the hard wood of the saloon floor. Morrie was still dazed by the earlier blow to his face and didn't react when Ross removed the gun from its holster and placed it on the bar. There was a brief silence, then all eyes were on the swing doors as they were pushed open by Marshal Waters. Ross was about to explain, but was taken by surprise when he saw that Marshal Waters was pointing a gun at him, even though Ross never carried a weapon.

'They asked for it, Marshal. Ross was just defending me,' explained Lisa who was still tenderly touching her face for any swelling that might have resulted from the blow she had received. The marshal raised his hand as a gesture that he wasn't interested in explanations.

'You can take care of yourself, Miss Lisa. Those two men

just rode into town for a quiet drink and Ross must have picked on them. Look what a state they're in. Someone go and fetch Doc Hannington to patch them up.'

The barman had already thrown a bucket of water over Deak, causing him to groan and then sit up. He had a vacant look on his face and winced when he rubbed his jaw. He spat some of his bloodied teeth on to the floor.

'If one of those drinks is yours, Ross, then you'd better knock it back because you'll be spending quite sometime behind bars. I warned you to stay out of trouble, but there's no getting through that thick skull of yours.'

Ross was still protesting his innocence ten minutes later when the door of his cell was slammed shut following the short walk across the street to the marshal's office. He hurled some choice words in the direction of the marshal as the lawman walked away.

When Ross had cooled down he tried to make himself comfortable on the hard bunk that hadn't been designed for someone of his size. He was thinking the marshal was getting cranky in his old age. Marshal Waters was usually one for having a quiet word and being a steadying influence, not for throwing men behind bars, unless it was for something serious. Sometimes he would lock men up for their own protection when he thought they'd had too much to drink.

Ross wished the marshal hadn't spoilt his last night in town, but he soon drifted off to sleep unaware that he wouldn't be leaving tomorrow. Tomorrow he would find out that he was in just the worst kind of trouble a man could be in.

THREE

Stephanie Shelton was leading the black stallion out of the stable when she saw the dust rising on the long, winding trail that led to the grand Shelton ranch house. She shielded her eyes from the sun and was relieved when she realized that the rider was her grandfather, Conrad Shelton. It seemed an age before he pulled up beside her and dismounted. He'd appeared worried and irritable when he'd ridden off with the men, but now he seemed pleased as she hugged him; she tried to hold back the tears, but couldn't.

'Something terrible has happened, Grandfather! I was just about to ride out and try to find you. It's about Daniel.'

'Daniel!' Shelton snapped, 'What's happened to your brother? I told you both to stay on the ranch and it looks as though you were going to disobey me if you were planning to go into town with that letter you're holding?'

'I'm not going to town, Grandfather. I told you I was going to look for you. This letter was delivered by a man just five minutes ago and he took Daniel. You must have passed them when you were riding in. He had a gun pointing at Daniel and forced him to go with him. It was all so horrible and I thought he might shoot Daniel when Daniel refused to go with him. I begged Daniel to do what the man wanted.'

Shelton's face flushed with anger and rage. 'I didn't see any riders. Why didn't any of the men stop this man?'

'All the men had gone off with you or were out with the herd and Joshua had taken two of the horses into town to the blacksmith's. He's only just come back. It all happened so quickly and that horrible man said that if I screamed he would kill Daniel and me. It was so terrifying.'

Stephanie's eyes filled with tears again and Conrad Shelton put his arm around his granddaughter. He would never be able to forget his dear wife, Constance, while his granddaughter was around. She had the same neat little nose, high cheekbones and lively smiling blue eyes. The light brown hair usually fell on to her shoulders, but was pinned back now as it always was when she went riding. Stephanie had blossomed into a lovely young woman and recently he'd had to warn some of the men to stop sniffing around. She was out of bounds to them, but he had no need to worry because she would soon be married to a man who was well suited to her, and he wasn't some common cowhand.

'Grandfather, the man said that you should open that letter as soon as you got back because it was very, very important. He seemed insistent. I didn't like him. He was so threatening towards Daniel, but he kept smiling when he looked at me. He made me feel uncomfortable.'

'Now, you go inside the house, honey, and ask cook to

18

make us some coffee. I'll be along as soon as I've sorted a few things out.'

Shelton watched Stephanie as she walked towards the house and then he led both horses into the stables.

Joshua Tyler had worked at the ranch for the last two years as a stable lad. He was slightly built, with large eyes that always appeared to be wide-open with excitement like a child at Christmas. His ma worked as a cleaner for the Sheltons and she still treated him like a little boy, but he never objected. He smiled at Conrad Shelton as he took the reins of his horse.

'I'll give yours a special rub down, Mr Shelton.'

'Make sure you do, but do it later,' Shelton growled. 'I want you to ride to town, go into the saloon and tell Foley to get himself and all the men back here as quick as their horses will carry them. And tell Foley I don't want them finishing their drinks first. This is urgent. Do you understand?'

Joshua gave a nervous reply and then reached for the reins of one of the horses that he'd just ridden back from the blacksmith's.

Conrad Shelton followed the stable lad outside and then waited for him to ride off before he ripped open envelope and pulled out the note which read:

We warned you not to come looking for your grandson. If you want to see him alive then it will cost you $20,000. You have seven days. When you have the money let your granddaughter's black horse run loose in the corral. We'll be in touch, but if you try anything or go running to the marshal we will brand your grandson with the Clarkson *brand and burn him and your granddaughter alive. You will remember the Clarkson brand, won't you? We might think about using Stephanie for pleasure before she turns to cinders.*

Shelton clenched his fists causing the note to be crumpled in his hand. His eyes scanned the distant scene as if he suspected that he was being watched. He hadn't heard the name Clarkson mentioned since he'd left Garman Creek nearly twenty years ago and it was a name he hadn't wanted to be reminded of.

Shelton was trying to calm himself before going into the house when he saw two of his men who had been guarding the herd ride up to the bunk house. He called them over. He ordered them stay on guard outside the house, telling them not to let any strangers come close to the house. They were to shoot anyone who didn't heed a warning to stay put and declare their business.

'What's happened, Mr Shelton?' one of the men asked, but was told to mind his own business and just follow his instructions by Shelton who then went inside the house.

Shelton was badly in need of a whiskey. He hurried to his oak-panelled study and poured a glass of his favourite brand of hard liquor. He mostly consumed liquor in moderation, but right now he needed a hefty drink and he kept the bottle within reach as he slumped into his chair and then took his first gulp. He'd already done some calculations in his head and was certain that he could raise the ransom for his grandson's release, but he might lose everything that he'd worked, and even killed, for. Perhaps if he raised most of the money without selling the ranch he could buy some time and maybe discover who was behind all this. Who could it be and what was the connection with the name Clarkson? His thoughts briefly turned to the Brock brothers who, he now knew, hadn't been involved in the first threats. He quickly dismissed any feelings of guilt about hanging them because as far as he was concerned they were lazy good for nothings and one of them had been lusting after Stephanie. There was also the question of their trespassing on Shelton land. He took another gulp of whiskey, then rubbed his hands through his thick grey hair. Before his thoughts turned to other matters he had convinced himself that he had done a public service by getting rid of the three brothers.

'There you are, Grandfather,' Stephanie sighed as she entered his study without knocking. 'Are you all right? What did the note say?'

'I'm just trying to decide whether it is some sort of prank. I'm thinking that that man could have been put up to it by friends of your brother's. Anyway, there's nothing for you to worry your pretty little head about. I have sent some men out to look for Daniel and I have told them to keep an eye out for any strangers. I'll get Foley to have some men patrol the approach to the ranch, just in case.' He hadn't mentioned the first note that had been left tucked into his horse's saddle a few days ago. Maybe Daniel's kidnappers would let him go when they found out what had happened to the Brock brothers.

'That man didn't look like the sort to take part in a prank and he was too old to be mixing with Daniel's friends,' countered Stephanie, who was totally unconvinced by her grandfather's assessment of her ordeal.

21

'If it isn't a prank, then I wouldn't be surprised if Ross isn't mixed up in it.'

Stephanie looked hurt at the suggestion, and retorted, 'You can't mean that, Grandfather! Steve would never do such a thing. Why do you still keep putting him down now that we're not seeing each other any more?'

Conrad Shelton regretted his condemnation of Ross and tried to make amends by saying, 'You are probably right, honey, and I suppose my dislike of the man clouds my judgement. You and Mark will make a perfect match and I should forget all about Steve Ross, just like you have.'

Stephanie wished that her grandfather was right, but she hadn't forgotten about Steve Ross and feared that she never would. If she did marry Mark Franklyn then it would be more to please her grandfather than to satisfy her own hopes of happiness.

FOUR

Ross had been awake since dawn. It hadn't been his first night in the town's cells, but it had been the most uncomfortable. The marshal had told him to expect some company when the Shelton cowhands got themselves fired up with liquor. He'd heard some gunshots before he drifted off to sleep, but the bed opposite his was still empty and he hadn't heard any grunting or snoring from the cell next door, so he guessed there hadn't been any serious trouble.

Marshal Waters didn't speak when he shoved Ross's breakfast under his cell door and then walked back to the office area.

Ross had never mastered the art of cooking and even this simple meal looked appetizing to him. He was mopping up the large portion of beans with a thick chunk of bread when the marshal reappeared and opened his cell.

'You'd best come with me, Ross, because I have some bad news for you. Let's go to the office and you can share some of my coffee that's just about brewed.'

The marshal looked as though he was about to break bad news to someone who had lost a dear one and waited until Ross had taken a few sips of the hot coffee before he spoke.

'You're in a heap of trouble, son, and I'm not sure that you deserve to be.'

'You're not serious, Marshal. You can't keep me locked up for that bit of scrapping over at the saloon. Those strangers were looking for trouble and one of them slapped Lisa. I can't abide a man who hits a woman and I'd have thought you'd be the same.'

'Ross, because of that little bit of scrapping, as you call it, that man who hit Lisa ended up dead. He might have been a son of a bitch, but you killed him and it don't matter none that you didn't intend to.'

Ross took a gulp of the hot coffee as the shocking news sunk in. He'd killed a man, but he still found it hard to believe. He eventually managed to speak.

'But he was all right when we left the saloon. You saw him yourself, Marshal. How can a man be like he was and then just die? You don't die from just maybe a broken jaw, because that's all he had.'

'Doc Hannington reckons he must have had a thin skull, because when they took him back to his surgery to patch him up he went all funny. His eyes rolled up and he died right in front of the doc.'

'But I just punched him. I didn't hit his head with a gun butt, or an iron bar,' Ross pleaded.

'Nothing you can say is going to change anything, Ross. The doc reckons he might have hit his head on the saloon floor. He mentioned something about a blood clot, but it all sounded too complicated for me. Anyway, you'd better get back in your cell. There'll be a trial, of course, and with a good lawyer you might escape a hanging, but you'll be an old man if ever you get out of prison.'

Ross was returned to his cell. He slumped down on to the bed and looked a forlorn figure as the marshal locked the cell door.

'You've just reminded me of the first time I killed a man. I take it this was your first, Ross.'

'Of course it was,' Ross shouted back, angry at the suggestion that he might have killed before. The marshal told him that shouting and hollering wasn't going to change anything and he reminded him that he'd brought it on himself.

Ross sat on his bed and held his head in his hands, confused and shocked as he tried to take in the news. That feller was a troublemaker, but he didn't deserve to die. Ross should have been saddling up about now, having said a few goodbyes, but instead he was in a mess. He couldn't face a long prison sentence locked away for who knew how many years. He would sooner hang than lose his freedom. At least he had no family to bring shame on. He'd never known his pa, and his ma had been killed by a drunken cowboy when she'd worked as a saloon girl. He'd only been twelve years old at the time and had run away from the town where it happened. He'd always been big for his age and he managed to get work on various farms until he'd arrived in Craigy Plains three years ago and worked for old man Tom Grainger. Tom had died last year when he'd fallen from his horse on his way back from town after filling himself full of hard liquor. Ross had found a

25

document that old Tom had had drawn up, all legal, in which he'd signed over the land to Ross.

It was early afternoon when the marshal brought him some food. Ross had decided that he would do his best to escape and hope not to do the old marshal too much harm in the process. He didn't know how he would manage it because the marshal might be long in the tooth, but he was a wily old so and so and he could still handle a gun as well as most men.

The marshal opened the cell door and passed him a plate of beans and some coffee. Ross was within a whisker of jumping the lawman, but he was taken aback when the Marshal told him to come and join him in the office after he'd finished his meal. He watched the marshal walk away, leaving the cell door open, and suddenly he didn't have any stomach for food. The marshal trusted him and that would make it easier to escape because now he planned to jump the marshal as soon as he got to the office. The marshal would be sitting down and it would make things easier. He would throw the hot coffee at the marshal and take him by surprise.

When Ross reached the office carrying his mug of hot coffee he was the one who was surprised. The marshal was sitting in his chair with his feet on his desk and he was pointing a gun at him.

'Come and sit down, son.' The marshal beckoned him towards a chair opposite his desk. 'If you are wondering what all that shooting was about yesterday, it was the Shelton boys. They were all celebrating something and old Conrad Shelton was paying for all they could drink. Then

Joshua, the Shelton stable lad, came riding down Main Street as though he was being chased by a pack of warmongering Indians and a few minutes later they all rode out of town.'

The marshal smiled and waved his pistol. 'This is just in case you try something stupid before I get a chance to run an idea by you. By the way, you had a couple of visitors earlier, but I turned them away. They brought you that pie there. It was Lily and Kathy who work for Lisa. I believe they are sisters and they told me to tell you that you can thank them when you get out. I didn't tell them that you wouldn't be getting out. They seemed too nice to be working in a saloon and too good for you, Ross.'

Ross was on the point of sitting down when he heard the office door open. The marshal turned his head and lowered his gun. Ross prepared to launch himself at the marshal, but stopped when he recognized who had just entered. It was Mark Franklyn a young lawyer who was working for Conrad Shelton and was expected to marry his granddaughter Stephanie.

Franklyn looked serious and apologized for interrupting them. Franklyn was immaculately dressed in a black suit and matching Stetson which looked out of place for a young man to be wearing in a town like Craigy Plains. He was just less than six feet tall and of slim build. His brown moustache was well groomed thanks to his daily visit to the barber's shop.

'Marshal,' said Franklyn, then paused. His eyes had fixed on the marshal's gun and he asked, 'Is everything all right here and, if it don't sound like a dumb question, why are you pointing your pistol at Steve?'

'Ross here is facing a murder charge, but I was about to put a proposition to him. Anyway, what brings you here, Mr Lawyer?'

'I heard that Steve was in trouble and came to offer him my help, but I didn't realize it was so serious.'

The marshal placed his pistol on the desk. 'I know you two are sort of buddies and you being a legal man you might want to listen in and perhaps be able to give him some advice,' he said.

'I'd be only too pleased to if that's what Steve wants.'

Steve greeted Franklyn and said he had no idea what the marshal was proposing, but he'd be grateful for any advice and then joked about providing it didn't cost anything. Franklyn shook hands with Ross, whom he had got to like after Ross had intervened when he was being picked on by a drunken cowboy in the saloon a few months earlier.

'I think I owe you one, Steve.'

The marshal invited Franklyn to take a seat and asked Ross not to interrupt while he outlined what he had in mind. The marshal explained what had happened over at the saloon, saying that that was why Ross was facing the prospect of a noose around his neck. The marshal put forward his proposal and in a casual tone asked Ross what he thought of the idea.

Ross shook his head and despite the seriousness of his predicament managed to smile before he replied, 'You want me to become your deputy and if I do I won't face charges for killing that man! You can't be serious, Marshal. For one thing I don't even carry a gun and what do I know about keeping the law?'

28

'I've got a hunch that you'd make a fine lawman with me to guide you, and don't worry about a gun. It don't matter none if you've never even fired one.'

Ross sighed, shook his head then said, 'But what about the trial?'

'There won't be any trial. Just to keep the paperwork straight I'll say that you were sworn in two days ago and you killed that troublemaker in the line of duty.'

Ross had doubt written all over his face before he spoke.

'I'm not sure,' said Ross. He turned to Franklyn. 'What do you think, Mark? It was a horrible accident and that's all. I didn't mean him to die and I've got witnesses.'

Franklyn took his time as he considered what the marshal had offered Ross. Then he had some advice for Ross.

'From the way the marshal described what happened and what I know of you, Steve, I have no doubts about it being an accident. If you turn down the marshal's offer I'll help you all I can. I could probably recommend someone to you and I think that with a decent defence lawyer and a reasonable jury you might get off with a light prison sentence, but it would be a gamble because juries can be unpredictable. The other thing is that you do have a bit of a reputation and that wouldn't be in your favour.'

'It looks as though I don't have much choice then,' Ross said with a sigh.

Marshal Waters looked pleased as he said, 'For a moment there I thought you were going to be a dumb young fool, but welcome aboard, son. We can dispense with all that swearing-in stuff.'

The marshal reached into his shirt pocket and took out a deputy marshal's badge. He tossed it on to the table towards Ross.

'And don't worry about not being able to handle a gun. I've got an idea about that and come tomorrow night, unless you've got two thumbs on your gun hand, you'll be a match for most men.'

Franklyn left the marshal's office, pleased that he had been able to return a favour to Ross. He'd been feeling guilty after he discovered that Ross and Stephanie had been sweethearts before he arrived, and but for Ross, he might have ended up dead, or severely beaten. Franklyn had problems of his own because of certain developments at the Shelton ranch. He had arrived in town just over six months ago after he was recommended to Conrad Shelton to do some short-term legal work. Then a romance had developed between him and Stephanie. There was talk of their getting married, but in recent weeks it had become obvious that Stephanie was unsure about their future together and there were other reasons why he knew that it would never happen.

FIVE

Lon Vickery patted his faithful dog, Boy, sitting beside him on the veranda of his small cabin which nestled beneath the south side of the Craigy mountain range, and looked towards the oncoming riders.

'Easy there, Boy. We haven't got anything worth stealing except you and you'd find your way back here. So, let's just wait and see what they want. If it's trouble then they can have it.'

Lon Vickery continued to pat the dog, but his right hand was gripping the pearl-handled pistol that was always within his reach.

'Howdy, Lon,' Marshal Waters shouted out as he pulled his horse up outside the cabin. 'I've brought my young deputy, Steve Ross, along. Thought we'd have a chinwag and enlist your help if you can spare us a few hours.'

Vickery had stood up. Now he moved his hand away from the pistol's handle and greeted the marshal. 'Come on in, Marshal. You're always welcome here.' He patted his dog again and whispered, 'It's friends, Boy, friends.' Boy stayed close to his master and still kept a watchful eye on their visitors.

It had been close to two months since the marshal had visited Lon. That had been a social call but this time he wanted a favour. Lon was nearing sixty years of age, but his shoulder length hair was jet black, as was his bushy, unkempt beard. Ross shook hands with the man who had become a legend in these parts, but he had never known he lived just five miles out of town.

Marshal Waters explained that he wanted Lon's help to teach Ross how to handle a pistol, but only if he would accept the two bottles of whiskey they'd brought for him.

'I'll do my best, Marshal, and I'm sure this young man will be a quick learner, but it will be quite a challenge we have if you're not pulling my leg when you say he's never even fired a gun. Well, that is unusual! I guess his ma and pa must have been God-fearing folk just like mine, because they couldn't abide violence of any kind. I was fourteen when I bought my first pistol and lied about my age, not that some storekeepers minded how old you were as long as you had the money.'

The marshal smiled and said, 'I don't think Ross took much notice of his folks preaching, if that was the case, because he has seen more than his share of violence, but we won't go into that. I'm not pulling your leg, Lon, about him never firing a gun before.'

Lon turned towards Ross. 'Then let's get to work, young Steve,' he said. 'I expect you think the old marshal is a bit weak in the head bringing you out all this way to be taught how to fire a gun by a blind man.'

Ross had been wondering about Lon, but he was still shocked to discover that he was totally blind. He would find out later that Lon's sight had been deteriorating for

32

many years. It had started while he was still acknowledged as having the fastest draw in Arizona and a few other states as well. It was rumoured that he had killed at least seventeen men, all of the killings had been in self-defence, but he would never comment on the actual number. He would always say that killing a man is never a thing to boast about.

'I'm going to have to get real close to you at times, son, so don't get too alarmed when I start feeling my way. First, I need to ask the marshal a few questions. Marshal, I take it you have seen Steve do a practice draw? So, how would you rate him on a scale of five? Putting modesty aside I would have placed me at a five, and probably you at a three when you were a bit younger, but you're probably a one now.' Lon laughed and added that he was joking about the marshal's decline in his ability to whip out his pistol at a decent speed.

'Well, I was going to say that's easy, Lon, and put him down at a one, but he's a bit erratic and sometimes he might make a three or even a four.'

Lon asked a few questions about the type of gun he was carrying, how low he was wearing it. Then he felt Ross's hand and tried estimating his height compared to his own. Lastly he asked Ross to hand him his pistol and did a series of checks and manoeuvres that included spinning and taking aim while he tried to assess its weight and balance.

'Before we start I'm going to ask the marshal to go into my cabin and bring out the Smith & Wesson, which is the fourth gun from the left in my gunrack.' Lon paused for a moment, pondering about his next choice for Ross before he decided, then he said, 'Just to the right of the gunrack you will see a rail with a collection of belts and holsters. Bring me the light brown one. That should suit him real fine.'

During the first session Lon concentrated on explaining to Ross the importance of how the holster was positioned to suit his own natural action. Then he explained something that made sense to Ross.

'I've know men try all combinations of how far the holster should be positioned down the leg without any regard to the length of their arms. Some scholarly type back East once did a study of men who had reputations for being quick on the draw. He thought he would come up with some mathematical formulae, but he discovered that no two were the same and that doesn't surprise me.'

Lon spoke at great length about the obvious importance of being accurate with the shot and ended by saying, 'There's no point in beating your opponent to the draw and then firing your shot into the saloon ceiling, or even have it whistle past his ear.'

By way of an exercise Lon asked the marshal to position two cans on the small fence in front of the cabin. Then he instructed Ross to stand close enough to one of them so that when he drew his pistol the barrel would strike the can. Then Lon, with the marshal's help, lined himself up with the other can.

'Now, son, holster your gun and let your gun hand take up its normal position. The marshal will count one, two, three and on a count of three we will draw as fast as we can.'

Ross just shook his head in amazement when Lon's can was struck ahead of his.

The exercise was repeated over and over. By the time they stopped Ross was beating Lon to the draw every time.

'I think that's enough for one day.' Lon laughed and then added, 'This young man is a natural. Being fast on the draw is mostly down to raw ability and a bit of technique. Don't take offence, Marshal, but you could practise every day of the week and you would never make a grade five.'

It was decided that target practice would be carried out elsewhere so as not to spook the horses and upset Boy, who had been watching the proceedings while looking a mite fed up. Ross thanked the old gunfighter for all his help, but Lon hadn't quite finished.

'I'll give you one final bit of advice, son, and that is to shoot between the eyes if you can and you think the man you're facing deserves to die, because it is vital for your survival. The body is obviously an easier target, but he might still get a shot off if you only wound him. It has to be a judgement about whether you should shoot to kill or wound, but I guess the marshal will teach you more about that than I can. Most of the men I called out, or who had challenged me, would probably have tried to come after me another time, or perhaps shoot me in the back. I have only ever wounded three men and they were young, drunken cowboys who wanted to show off in front of their friends, or maybe impress a saloon girl. They would likely piss in their pants the next day when they realized how close they had come to dying and, we hope, would never try anything so dumb ever again.'

Before they left Lon's place Ross got to see Lon's vast armoury of pistols that he'd used or collected over many years. His favourite weapon had been the Peacemaker, but his wrists had been stronger in his younger days and he said that it wouldn't be suitable now. Lon insisted that Ross kept the Peacemaker and holster that he had selected as a gift and said he would be offended if they tried to pay him for it.

On their way back to Craigy Plains, Ross and the marshal stopped for some target practice. Once again the marshal was mesmerized by Ross's ability and even began to wonder whether perhaps Ross had been less than truthful about his past. After they mounted up and continued their journey, the marshal was thinking that on reflection there had to be a good reason why a man wouldn't carry a gun to protect himself, unless he was a man of the cloth. The marshal gave a quiet chuckle at the thought of Ross being a Bible punching preacher. Well, he could certainly punch!

'What's tickled you, Marshal? I don't recall seeing you laugh. A smile maybe, but that's all. So, are you going to share it with me?' Ross asked.

'I was just wondering if you had ever been a preacher. I know you don't go to church, but maybe that's because you became disillusioned?'

Ross laughed at the marshal's suggestion and said, 'I think all that gunfire back there might have scrambled your old brain, Marshal. What made you think such a thing? Now, if you'd asked me if I'd ever been a bank-robber that might be different.'

'So have you ever been a bank-robber?'

'I'm not going to answer that, Marshal. Why don't you have another look through all those wanted posters when we get back to the office? Now let's have a race back to town because my dry mouth is craving for a beer. Right! Let's go!'

Ross galloped away at speed. The marshal shook his head, smiled and kept his horse moving at the same pace. He was pleased with the way things had gone out at Lon's place. Like all old marshals he relied upon his gut feelings about some things. He had a feeling that Ross was going to be a fine lawman and he hoped he was right because he had real bad vibes about trouble brewing and heading his way.

SIX

Tommy Maben wondered whether anyone would recognize him as he eased the dark-brown mare into a gentle trot when he entered Craigy Plain's Main Street. He'd heard about the railroad coming to the town and how it had prospered. He could see Monckton's general store was still there and Jacko's barber shop. The Elm House saloon looked as though it had recently been given a fresh lick of paint and it had been extended. He had always wondered what it was like inside the saloon, and intended to find out, but not today. The bank was new and so was the Sheelagh Tequila's diner. Doc Hannington's surgery was another building that had been spruced up and, although his name was displayed above the door, he thought the old doc had probably retired by now or gone to join some of his patients in the cemetery.

Maben was twenty years old, and his six foot frame was powerfully built. He wasn't a man who smiled often and his blue eyes were cold and mostly threatening to anyone who met them.

He was thinking that perhaps it had been a mistake to

come into town, but he didn't have much choice now that his food supplies had run out. It had been a week since he'd returned to the rundown farmhouse that had been his home until he was a twelve-year-old boy. Some men would have cried when they saw inside the cabin, which was exactly like it was when he'd left it nearly eight years ago. His ma's picture was a little faded and his pa's pipe was on the table. He'd heard a scuttling sound that told him he wasn't alone, but he would soon get rid of the rats.

Maben rode by the marshal's office and remembered Marshal Waters. He'd liked the marshal because he'd been kind to the family when they had been in trouble, but he'd still kill him if he had to. He wouldn't be the first lawman he'd killed. Perhaps it was just as well that his old ma wasn't still alive. She wouldn't understand the life he'd led, or what he was intending to do. She always looked for the best in people. Sorry, Ma, but life isn't like that. Life is cruel and you have to be cruel to survive. He wished his pa hadn't been so weak, but he didn't blame him for what had happened.

He pulled up outside Monckton's store, but was drawn to the sign outside the Elm House saloon, to which he was now close enough to see that it read: *We have the best beer and girls in Arizona. Come and sample both.* The faintest of smiles appeared on his weather-beaten face. He would give his non-shooting arm for a glass of beer and a buxom woman right now. He would have done what he intended to do within a week and then he could think about enjoying himself and getting on with his life. Perhaps some of the bitterness that had warped his view of life would leave him, but he wouldn't become a preacher like his ma had wanted him to be. He'd done things that no God could ever forgive and he hadn't finished yet!

Norman Monckton greeted him with a friendly smile, but didn't appear to show any indication that he recognized him. Maben had already prepared what he would say if anyone did and was confident that he could convince anyone that he was Deano Brady and had never been in this town until today. He told Monckton that he needed to stock up on food, but he would mosey around the store for a while in case he spotted something else that he wanted. The layout of the store was just as he remembered it when he came to town with his ma and the candy jar was in the same position. Perhaps he'd lingered too long in front of it and that was what prompted Monckton to say, 'You remind me of someone, but I can't think who. Have you got kinfolk in these parts?'

After Maben had delivered his prepared response Monckton had an explanation for thinking he looked familiar.

'It must be the clothes that you young fellers wear that makes you look so alike to me. Anyway, what can I get you today? I've had some fancy shirts just come in and you can have one at a special price seeing as how you are my first customer of the day.'

Maben remembered his ma saying that Norman Monckton could sell snow to the Eskimos and he obviously hadn't changed, judging by his sales patter. He told Monckton that he wasn't one for wearing anything fancy and then reeled off his list of food requirements and treated himself to some soap and a few other bits and pieces. Monckton asked if he was staying in these parts.

Maben lied again and said that he was just passing through. He could sense that Monckton was studying him so, once his purchases were packed, he left the store. He was about to mount his horse when a rider pulled up outside the saloon. He'd put on a bit of weight from what Maben remembered, but it was definitely him. He wasn't the man he'd come back to kill, but he probably would take care of Ed Foley as well if he got the chance. But not just yet. Maben wanted to revive some old memories, the pleasant ones, before he did what he'd planned for so long. Then he would never set foot in this town ever again.

Norman Monckton was soon following Maben out of his store to sweep away the dust from Main Street off the sidewalk outside the shop. He watched Maben head out of town. He might never have given him a second thought had he not just seen him again. Deano, or whatever he called himself, was the spitting image of Hal Maben, or at least the young Hal Maben. Monckton's usually cheery face took on a sad look for a moment when he recalled what had happened to poor Hal. Monckton's wife had received a few letters from Alice Maben after she'd moved to her sister's in Lincoln, Northern Arizona. She'd said that she would visit one day, but she never did, probably because it was over 300 miles away. Then, two years ago, her son Tommy had written a short letter saying that his ma had passed away. Tommy had been a fiery sort of lad, big for his age and fond of fighting. Monckton had wondered how Tommy had turned out as a young man.

SEVEN

'How far have we got to go, Marshal?' Ross asked as they rode beside the undertaker's wagon.

'Not much more than half a mile if that feller gave us the right directions.'

'I've never seen anyone so spooked as that poor feller. He looked pale just recounting the tale,' said Ross.

'I don't want you puking on me, boy, if you haven't seen a dead man before,' the marshal teased.

'Don't worry, Marshal. I've seen my share of dead cattle that were all skin and bone because of the drought, or had had the innards ripped out by wolves or something bigger.'

'I hope you're right, Ross, but you might be in for a shock, just like that feller was who stumbled on those bodies. From the way he described the location they might never have been found. He didn't say what he was doing in that clearing, but I don't suppose it matters. Some folks would have just got the hell out of there and not bothered reporting it.'

Luke Mason, assistant to Abraham Tweedie, the

42

undertaker, had been listening to the lawmen's conversation as he was driving the wagon. It had caused him to smile because he doubted if they were going to see anything that he hadn't seen before.

The rest of their journey to a spot just three miles from town was conducted in silence until the marshal told them they were there. He directed his horse through a gap in the trees. When they entered the clearing the marshal clapped his hands together, but one hungry vulture was determined to have a last tug at the piece of flesh that was in its beak. The marshal drew his pistol and fired a shot above the trees. The large bird screeched and flew off in the direction his companions had taken.

Luke Mason had been wrong about his preparedness for what they were going to encounter. When he caught sight of the three mutilated and headless bodies hanging from the trees he turned away and began retching. He managed to hold back the puke long enough to save his professional reputation, at least for now.

Ross didn't flinch at the gruesome sight and the marshal was the first to speak when he said, 'Jesus Christ, what sick son of a bitch did that to these poor souls? And what could they have done to deserve suffering like they must have endured?'

Luke Mason had recovered sufficiently to look at the bloodied flesh, and he gave his opinion about what might have happened. 'It must have been some Indian raiding party.'

The marshal gave the young assistant a sympathetic look and advised, 'Mason, you stick to undertaking because you're sure as hell not much good at detective work. There isn't an Indian within five hundred miles of here and they are all law-abiding and living in peace on a reservation. You best bring your wagon closer in here so we can cut down these poor souls, or what's left of them, and take them back to town so that you and your boss can prepare them to be buried.'

While Mason positioned the wagon beneath the hanging corpses the marshal stood and studied the naked remains of the three men. They hadn't been the first men to hang from these trees because the barks were badly scuffed with marks that had been caused by the spurs of previous victims who had tried to pull themselves back to the trees. He was thinking that if they had been wearing some clothes it might have provide some means of identification. It was clear that they had all been young men and two of them had been muscular. Only the third one retained some part of his manhood that hadn't been ripped away. Maybe someone would report them missing because otherwise their identity would likely remain a secret.

'Marshal, come and see this,' Ross called out from the other side of the clearing to where he had wandered off.

The marshal was deep in thought as he continued to inspect the bodies.

'Marshal, over here,' Ross called out, louder this time.

'Jesus, that's Joey Brock, and some sick son of a bitch has stuck a cigar butt in his mouth,' said the marshal when he looked down into the small grave that Ross had uncovered. Ross had already brushed aside the worms on the face, but some had returned and seemed to be interested in Joey's eyes, apart from the one that had

44

crawled up inside his nose.

'You'd better look in those two,' ordered the marshal after he'd seen the other two mounds of earth.

Ross quickly dug out the top layer with his bare hands, but was more careful when he got close to the face. Even the marshal grimaced and Mason, who had just walked over quickly hurried away and this time he did puke.

'That's Brad, isn't it?' asked Ross. Brad was the only one of the Brock brothers he had met and that was when they had brawled outside the saloon not more than a month ago. Ross remembered it being a close fight until he had delivered a couple of heavy blows to Brad's belly.

'It's Brad all right, but he had two good eyes when he was in the saloon just a couple of days ago. I guess you'll uncover Mickey in the last one because the brothers mostly travelled together except when they were sniffing around after a woman.'

The marshal could see that Ross was struggling with digging out the last grave and he suggested that Mason should take over, but when he took a closer look at Mason he decided that it probably wasn't a good idea. Mason's face was as white as a sheet and instead the marshal advised him to go and sit on the wagon.

Ross was breathing heavily when he stood up. 'I've dug down further than the other two, Marshal, and there's no sign of anything.'

'Right, let's get these bodies loaded and get out of here. Perhaps an animal carried the head away and someone filled the hole in, although I can't see why they'd bother.'

Mason had recovered sufficiently to help lower the bodies on to the wagon where they were carefully laid

45

beside each other. Ross used some canvas from the wagon to wrap the heads in and placed them near the bodies. He was still puzzled about finding nothing in the third small grave. He headed back to it and started digging deeper.

'Come on, Ross, let's get going. You won't find anything in there.' The marshal called out just as Ross was pulling out the third head. It might have been hacked from the body of Mickey Brock, but there was no way of knowing because the face had been battered beyond recognition. Ross wrapped it in another piece of canvas to spare Mason the ordeal of seeing it and told the marshal about the state it was in. The strange thing was that the flattened face had not attracted the attention of the worms like the other two.

Doctor Samuel J. Hannington was seventy-two years of age, a small, dapper man, who had never married and had been the town's first and only doctor. He'd seen his share of tragedy and victims of the Civil War, but none more gruesome than the remains of the three men who were now laid out on makeshift tables in his small surgery. The Brock brothers had no relatives that anyone knew about so they at least would be spared having to see them laid out in their coffins. Doc Hannington was certain that Abraham Tweedie would do his best for the two men who still had a recognizable face when he prepared them for burial. The doc scribbled down some notes as to the nature of the wounds as Marshal Waters looked on. There was a particular pattern on all three which indicated that the vultures must have shared a preference for certain parts of the body.

The smallest of the three men had had less of his flesh torn away. His was the last of the bodies that the doc was inspecting when he shook his head and said, 'Well I'll be damned. This isn't Mickey Brock. There's only one birthmark like that in the whole wide world. Marshal, I'm afraid you'll be riding out to the Shelton ranch to deliver some heartbreaking news.'

EIGHT

Stephanie had ridden the black stallion hard before she pulled it up near her favourite spot on the hillside. Grandfather would be furious if he found out that she'd ridden out here alone, but she couldn't stand being cooped up in the ranch and she was a young woman, not a child. On a clear day she could see the Craigy mountain range in the distance, but today the hazy sky meant that she could only see down into the valley and the fast-flowing Sturm River. She had much to think about because she had promised to tell Mark Franklyn in two days' time whether she would agree to marry him.

Her grandfather was trying to put on a brave face, but she knew that he was as worried as she was. It had been three days since she had seen Daniel being taken away and she knew that her brother's disappearance was not a prank, as Grandfather tried to pretend it was.

Grandfather would be thrilled if she decided to accept Mark's proposal because he had made it clear that Mark had his approval. Mark was older than she was, but handsome, although he wasn't a rugged-looking man. He was sensitive and gentle, but being a legal and financial man he had no call to be like those other men she saw around the ranch, or even like Steve Ross. Some of her friends drooled over Mark, especially Dorothy Toms, but there was something missing in her feelings for him.

If only Grandfather wasn't so set against Steve Ross then she could be looking forward to marrying him instead of dithering about Mark Franklyn. She had only seen Steve from a distance during the eight months since their tearful parting and she didn't know whether he still had strong feelings for her. She had heard talk that he was sweet on Marielou, the saloon girl. She'd only seen Marielou just the once and she was the sort that would make any man's head turn. Stephanie had felt her heart sink when she overheard some of the cowhands talking about Steve's intention to leave if the drought didn't end soon.

Stephanie wished her grandfather didn't bare grudges the way he did, or feel so much anger towards Steve just because he wouldn't sell him his land. Some of the landowners had given in to her grandfather, but Steve Ross wasn't the sort to give into a bully and that was what Grandfather could be sometimes. He had tried to turn her against Steve again just yesterday when he said that he had killed a man in a saloon brawl, but Mark had told her that it had been an accident and that Steve had become a deputy marshal.

Stephanie was only eighteen years old. She had known Mark Franklyn such a short time and she wished the mother whom she had never known was here now to advise her on such things. Stephanie's parents, Conrad

Junior and Eve had died when their train came off its tracks when they were visiting kinfolk back East. Stephanie and her twin brother, Daniel had been three years old and she had vague memories of Grandmother Shelton, who had helped raise them until she died from the fever when they were just seven years old. She and her brother had then been brought up by a series of governesses while living with their grandfather, who had always seemed too busy to pay them much attention.

Stephanie dearly wished that her grandfather would stop trying to control her life, but she hoped that he'd been around to notice the unwelcome attention that she had been receiving from Ed Foley. The ranch foreman was old enough to be her father and he had a wife, but he had been making flattering remarks, some of them had been suggestive and had made her blush. She mostly wore long clothes when out riding, but whenever they met she felt, from the way his eyes studied her, as though he was undressing her. She had always been self-conscious about her large breasts ever since she'd developed them as a young girl and his staring at them made her feel uncomfortable. He had once remarked that she was the most womanly thing he had ever seen and Mark Franklyn was going to be the luckiest man on earth. She tried her best to laugh off his remarks, but they were becoming more daring and personal.

She gave a heavy sigh and her thoughts turned to her brother Daniel. Daniel had only returned home recently and he had told her about his concern over their grandfather's plans to groom him to take over the ranch. Daniel had not the slightest interest in the ranch and had been so disappointed when Grandfather had refused to give him the money so that he could travel abroad. Daniel liked the fine things in life and was just not cut out to be a rancher, but Grandfather had told him that he was a Shelton and ranching was in his blood. Daniel was even more concerned when he heard that Grandfather wanted him to move out of the house and sleep in the bunkhouse with the other men and have his meals with them. Daniel's generous allowance was going to be stopped and he would be paid the same as the other junior cowhands. Grandfather had told him that he would have the time of his life and it would be better than mixing with those weak wastrels he'd met back East.

Daniel had already made plans to leave home, but she wondered how he would be affected by his experience of being kidnapped. Stephanie had even considered the possibility that Grandfather was behind Daniel's kidnap, but she now feared that she might never see her brother again unless her grandfather stopped being stubborn and faced up to the seriousness of the threat.

Stephanie's struggles with her problems had tired her and she had drifted off to sleep with her head resting on the small slope beneath the tree. When she awakened it took a while for her to remember where she was. She thought she was dreaming until she became aware of a figure on horseback staring down at her. She wasn't alarmed at first, thinking that it was a ranch hand who had been sent after her by her grandfather. The man's face was familiar when he smiled. She feared that it might be Ed Foley and now she wished it was because it was actually the man who had taken Daniel away. Her eyes darted towards her own horse and the rifle in the scabbard, but she dismissed any thoughts of trying to reach it. She slowly got to her feet and tried to calm herself. She decided to pretend that she didn't know the man and said,

'You must be lost. This is private land.'

The man sneered and replied, 'I'm not lost, Stephanie. I've come to talk to you and to ask you to pass a message to your silly grandpa. Tell him that the clock's ticking and his time's running out if he wants to see your brother again, alive I mean. Now you tell him that. By the way, I've been watching your lovely body move up and down as you were breathing. You must have been dreaming about something, because you were sighing and moaning like a saloon girl being pleasured by a horny cowboy. I was hoping you were going to sleep longer. Perhaps I'll just take a closer look at you.'

Stephanie watched as he started to dismount, then she raced towards her horse which was grazing nearby, with its reins dangling free. She had never been more terrified in her whole life as she mounted her horse and then felt the man's hand grab her riding-boot.

NINE

Conrad Shelton was in a foul mood when Mark Franklyn arrived in his study. He had just been told that his granddaughter had disobeyed his orders and gone riding by herself.

'I hope you can tame that granddaughter of mine when you are married because she can be as disobedient as an untrained stallion.'

Mark Franklyn smiled, but didn't comment, preferring to report on his findings.

Shelton had instructed him to make arrangements to sell any assets in the way of investments that he held and now he was studying the figures on the sheet that Franklyn had handed him.

'You are a very wealthy man, sir, and possibly the richest in the state of Arizona.'

'What you see there, Mark, is the result of many years' hard work. Yes, I've had my share of luck, but there have been hard times, like now with the current drought, but fortunately I am well covered to cope with that thanks to our own water supply from the Sturm River. Others aren't so lucky and that's why I'm raising this money so I can buy up some of the ranches at a knockdown price.'

Conrad Shelton had still to decide whether he would pay the ransom money, or use it for the purpose which he had just told Franklyn it was intended for, but he was thinking that it was very unlikely he would hand over his money to any kidnappers.

'That's very, shrewd, sir. By the way, is there any news of Daniel? Stephanie was telling me that you think he's the victim of some sort of prank.'

'She wasn't supposed to tell anyone, but I guess you are a bit special, so it doesn't matter. He met up with a strange crowd who have nothing better to do than spend their folks' money and it's probably their way of having a bit of fun. He'll be home soon.'

Their conversation was interrupted by the sound of gunfire which caused Shelton to jump and then hurry towards the door, but not before he had taken a pistol from the drawer of his desk.

He was greeted by one of his men who had just ridden up to the house, who called out to him.

'It's all right, Mr Shelton. One of the men was just being careful. One of those riders heading in is Marshal Waters.'

Shelton squinted into the bright sunlight at the riders heading towards the house. He ordered his men to show the marshal into his study when he arrived, then he made his way back inside with Franklyn following close behind him.

Shelton looked troubled when they returned to his study. He poured himself a whiskey, drank it, and said, 'I can't think what would bring the marshal out all this way.'

He was about to refill his glass with whiskey, but stopped when he heard the knock on the door and Marshal Waters entered with Ross following close behind.

'What's Ross doing here, Marshal?' Shelton questioned with anger in his voice, 'I heard he killed a man not more than a week ago.'

'Ross is my deputy, Mr Shelton, and that killing was an accidental death.'

Shelton shook his head and then asked the marshal what brought him out to the ranch.

'I am the bearer of bad news, Mr Shelton. There's been a lynching. It was no ordinary lynching and the young man's face was unrecognizable, but Doc Hannington has identified him and that's why we're here.'

The blood drained from Shelton's face. 'The bastards, I'll make certain they pay for this, every last one of them.'

Marshal Waters and Ross exchanged surprised glances. The marshal was about to ask Shelton a question when the study door was flung open and a distraught Stephanie entered the room with tears streaming down her face.

Shelton rose quickly from his desk and hugged his granddaughter. He hadn't noticed her torn dress.

'What's happened, my dear? Have you heard the news about Daniel?'

Stephanie's distress was even greater as she asked, 'What's happened to Daniel? I have just been chased by that man who delivered the note and took Daniel away. I fell asleep when I was resting up on the hill and when I woke up he was standing there, but I managed to get away from him. He tried to pull me from my horse.'

Shelton hugged her again, then released her before he said in as calm a voice as he could muster, 'The marshal is here to deliver some bad news, so we've got to be brave.'

Marshal Waters looked uncomfortable and cleared his throat.

'It's about Daniel, isn't it?' Stephanie blurted out. Mark Franklyn tried to hug her, but she broke free and appeared embarrassed as she looked towards Ross.

Marshal Waters sighed heavily before he spoke.

'I think there may be some misunderstanding here, Mr Shelton. I've come to tell you that one of your cowhands has been found murdered along with two of the Brock brothers in rather gruesome circumstances. I wanted to tell you before we break the news to his ma. I take it that Martha still works for you.'

Some of the anxiety was gone from Shelton's face and he tried to sound sincere when he said, 'Why that's just terrible, Marshal. I knew the boy was missing, but I assumed he'd gone away for a while to rid himself of his mother's apron strings. His mother will be devastated and so will the cowhands. He was a popular boy.'

'Mr Shelton, what's all this about a note and your son Daniel?' enquired the marshal. 'It sounds as though he might be in some sort of danger. Is there anything you want to tell us in case we might be able to help?'

'Let's just say it's a private matter, Marshal. I thank you for your concern, but I grew up in an age when we took care of our own problems without relying on any help from the law.'

Ross's eyes met Stephanie's. He could tell that she wanted to say something, but when she did it wasn't what he'd expected.

'Deputy Ross, I'm glad you have taken up your new job. Mark told me how you saved him from a beating, and you'll be a great help to Marshal Waters.'

Ross smiled back at her, but felt awkward talking so formally to the woman he still loved when he replied, 'I'm still getting used to it, but I appreciate your kind words.'

Marshal Waters cleared his throat again, which was a habit he'd developed when speaking in awkward situations. He said that they would like to go and break the news to Tim Aitkin's ma.

The marshal turned round when he reached the doorway of the study and delivered an unwelcome message to Henry Shelton.

'Oh, and Mr Shelton, I'd like to speak to some of your cowhands to see if they can give any reason why young Aitkin would have been found with the Brock brothers. We'll be looking out for Mickey Brock as well, because he will be in for one hell of shock when he discovers what happened to his brothers.'

Shelton told the marshal that he was welcome to speak to any of his men if it could help, but he frowned when Ross asked Stephanie if she could describe the man who had chased her. Ross noted her anxiety when she looked towards her grandfather before she replied that there was nothing special about the man or his horse that she could remember.

Ross and the marshal had left Aitkin's ma being consoled by a visiting friend. Ross was thinking that breaking bad news wasn't a part of the job he was going to handle very well. Their visit to the bunkhouse to question the cowhands about Aitkin's disappearance didn't help much except to confirm that they were hiding something, just like Conrad and Stephanie Shelton. Marshal Waters' parting words to Ed Foley were to tell him that he would be back and wanted to see some of the men who were away managing the herd.

Ed Foley had seen Conrad Shelton explode into a wild rage on many occasions and when he entered his boss's study he knew he was about to witness another outburst.

Shelton made his usual threat to have Foley run off his ranch and then he would make certain that Foley never worked for anyone else, if he couldn't explain why Mickey Brock wasn't found hanging alongside his brothers.

'Mickey Brock is dead, Mr Shelton, and you have my word on that. I've never lied to you and I'm not now. When I chopped that good for nothing's head off I battered his face so badly that no one would ever recognize him. The marshal told me some cock-and-bull story about Doc Hannington recognizing a birth mark on one of the bodies and that's why they think it was young Aitkin. Well, the doc and the marshal are going to look like dumb fools when Aitkin comes back here to visit his ma.'

Conrad Shelton took a gulp of whiskey and stared hard into Foley's eyes.

'You'd better not be bullshitting me, Foley!' Shelton threatened once more.

'I wouldn't do that, sir, not with you. We go back a long way and you know how much respect I have for you. You should know by now that no man could be more loyal than I am to you. I owe you a lot and I'll never forget that.'

'All right,' said Shelton after a long pause, then he added, 'Talking of going back a long way, have you ever mentioned the Clarksons to anyone?'

Foley appeared surprised at the question and answered, 'No, never. What happened back there all those years ago is something that I try to forget and I haven't mentioned it to another living soul, but why do you ask after all this time?'

Shelton frowned and replied, 'It's just that the name came up recently and I thought you might have been blabbing about it to someone and giving them ideas. Anyway, I don't want the marshal snooping around after Aitkin. If that kid is out there, you find him and get him back here. And make sure that the men who helped string up the Brocks keep their mouths shut. Now you'd better get on with some work and tell the men to keep looking out for any strangers snooping around the place.'

When Foley reached the door Shelton called after him,

'Oh, and Foley, get an urgent message to that fellow who took care of that problem we had with the dumb ass who tried to recruit some of my men. I think I'll take out some insurance in case the marshal connects the Brocks's hangings to me, or some drunken cowboy has a loose tongue.'

Foley was pleased to hear that Shelton was being cautious, because he would be in big trouble as well if news of his involvement in the Brock brothers' deaths got out.

'I heard he's hanging around in Corrando Springs, the old mining town. I could get him here by tomorrow if I send one of the men for him.'

Shelton said, 'Good,' and reached for the whiskey bottle.

TEN

It was five days since the kidnappers had made their demand. After they had taken their breakfast together Conrad Shelton told Stephanie to leave her horse in the corral to signal to Daniel's kidnappers that he was ready to pay the ransom. He hadn't gathered the money, but he was confident that when the time came to hand over the ransom he could spring a trap. He ordered his men to keep off the approaches to the ranch so the kidnappers wouldn't be suspicious.

Stephanie's stallion had been in the corral for less than hour when Mark Franklyn arrived for a meeting with Shelton. He had brought with him an unexpected delivery. It was an envelope addressed to Conrad Shelton. It caused the rancher to look troubled as he sat in his large leather chair in his study studying the unopened envelope before he spoke.

'It's from them. How did you get this?' he demanded, clearly surprised that Franklyn would deliver it, although he hadn't expected the kidnappers to risk riding up to the ranch in person.

'I nearly didn't see it. It was pinned to a post on the entrance to the ranch. How do you know it's from them? I assume you mean Daniel's kidnappers.'

'How do you think! I recognize the handwriting and who else would it be from?' Shelton snapped back at Franklyn as he ripped open the envelope. He slowly read the instructions in the letter, already forming plans in his mind that would see the safe return of his grandson and the downfall of the kidnappers. Soon the hatred he had built up for whoever was behind this would be replaced by the satisfaction he would get from punishing them.

After a little time Shelton revealed the contents of the letter to Franklyn, who had stood watching the fury on Shelton's face change to a strange smile.

'They want us to drop the money off at the old sheltering cabin down by the river at three o'clock tomorrow. It says that I've got to go alone. Daniel will be there and they'll set him free once they've checked all the money has been handed over.'

Franklyn looked concerned when he said, 'Mr Shelton you won't be able to raise the money by that time tomorrow. I explained to you that it would take at least three days from the time you gave me the go-ahead. I thought you wanted the money to buy out the farmers hit by the drought?'

Shelton laughed out loud. 'That's exactly what I still plan to do. I won't be paying out my hard-earned money on any ransom demand. My men will be hiding out and we'll give these bastards what they deserve. When I say we, I mean me, because I'll be doing my own dirty work this time.'

Franklyn looked serious and tried to find the right words to express his concern.

'Mr Shelton, is it wise to try and trick them? These men don't seem the sort to mess about with, and remember they might harm Stephanie as well.'

Shelton glared at Franklyn and for a moment it seemed he would give him a tongue-lashing and tell him to keep his chicken-livered advice to himself.

'I think I know how to handle these no-goods, Franklyn. They're just bullies and bullies are usually cowards at heart. I'll tell you something else; these men are stupid or they don't know Conrad Shelton, or perhaps they think I've gone soft. I'm going to catch these varmints and when I do they'll wish they'd died like the Brock brothers did when they realize what I've got planned for them. When word gets out what happened to them my family will never be threatened by anyone ever again. I am a great believer in making an example of people who go against me.'

'Who are the Brock brothers, Mr Shelton? I was here the other day when Marshal Waters mentioned them.'

Shelton was preoccupied with other things and answered in a matter of fact fashion, 'They were cattle rustlers and perverts, that's who they were. I thought they were mixed up in these threats to my family, but they got what they deserved.'

'Forgive me for questioning you about Stephanie's safety, sir, but she's a beautiful young woman and some men are no better than animals. They see something they like and they just take it, if you get my meaning.'

'I do, Franklyn, and I expect your support on this, especially if there is any hint of danger to Stephanie.'

'I'm not what you call a fighting man, Mr Shelton. I don't even carry a gun, but I wouldn't let anyone harm Stephanie. You have my word on that,' replied Franklyn.

'I wasn't suggesting otherwise, Franklyn, but I think you have probably led a sheltered life coming from back East. You did say that you have no kinfolk, didn't you?'

'Yes, sir. My parents both died of some mystery illness when I was very young. I was lucky I survived because it killed my brother and sister as well.'

'That's a damned shame. Some folks get more than their fair share of grief, including myself suffering the loss of my only son and then my dear wife. Anyway, let's not be all maudlin. Best we get on with the business that brought you here.'

Shelton and Franklyn soon finished their discussions and, as Shelton watched Franklyn leave, he wondered about him. This was still a harsh land to live in and he wouldn't always be around to look out for Stephanie. No doubt Franklyn meant well with his assurances that he would take care of Stephanie, but he was too damned soft. The main thing was, he would make a better suitor than Ross, who had disrespected him by turning down a good offer for his land. Well, Ross would soon be selling it for peanuts if the drought lasted much longer.

Shelton was looking forward to tomorrow and the meeting with at least one of the kidnappers who had had the audacity to threaten him and his family. Perhaps the person behind the demands wouldn't be there, but by the time Shelton had finished torturing whoever came to collect the ransom he would know who it was. His experience had shown that a man could withstand any amount of pain, but how would they handle the threat of having their manhood cut off or their eyes poked out. He made a note to remember that tomorrow, and to give Daniel an opportunity to prove he was a man by administering some of the torture on his captor. Shelton was ready for his dinner. He hadn't felt this invigorated for a long time.

ELEVEN

Conrad Shelton steered his horse off the main trail and down towards the sheltering cabin and his anticipated reunion with his grandson. His saddle-bags were stuffed with paper and not the dollar bills the kidnappers were hoping to get their hands on. He reminded himself to act as normally as possible and not to look behind him in the direction of where his men were hiding, waiting for his signal to gallop down the slope towards the cabin and take care of the scum who had threatened his family. Shelton doted on Stephanie, but Daniel was special to him too. He had been educated back East and in some ways he was too soft, just like Mark Franklyn, with a woman's hands and no scars on his face, but he was a Shelton. He had returned home only a few days before he was kidnapped and Shelton hadn't had time to start on his plans to toughen him up. God willing, Daniel would one day carry the name Shelton on to greater things, but he had a lot of living and fighting to do before then. When all this was over Shelton planned to pay one of his men to take a beating off Daniel to build up his confidence. He also needed to sow his oats and enjoy life before being groomed for the responsibility of taking over running the ranch when Shelton retired. He would make sure that Lisa arranged a couple of nice girls for him, perhaps those sisters, Kathy and Lily.

Shelton studied the surrounding area. He could hear the fast flowing river that was no more than a hundred yards behind the cabin. He could see the bridge that he had built some years ago and now he was wishing that he'd stationed some men on the other side of the river. He felt a sense of relief when he spotted the blurred face through the small window, but the window was dirty and he couldn't see him clearly or hear what he was shouting. In a few minutes he would be hugging his grandson and telling him that there was going to be one hell of a party tonight. Then he saw the smoke coming from under the door and he fell from his horse in his haste to get inside the cabin. He felt the excruciating pain as he twisted his ankle, which caused him to hobble up the few steps on to the veranda. Then he rammed the door with his full weight, but it wouldn't give way despite his repeated attempts. He drew his pistol and fired a signal for his men to ride in. He made one final attempt before he struggled towards the small window, hoping to see his grandson and tell him that help was on the way. The smoke had grown thicker and he could feel the heat through the glass. He decided that he could wait no longer and used the butt of his pistol to smash the glass. He was forced back as the flames rushed towards him, but not before he had heard the terrified screams from within the cabin.

'Help him, damn it. Get the hell down here now,' Shelton cried out, expecting the men to be able to hear him. He turned to see them getting closer, but still some way off. He heard the whoosh as the fire inside raged on. The flames were now in the roof. He cried like a baby, mostly with despair as he heard the terrified screaming from inside, 'Help me. Help me.'

Conrad Shelton realized that his grandson must have been secured in some way and was unable to move. There was only one way that he could help his grandson now. He fired through the broken glass into the flames that had completely engulfed the shaking and blazing figure inside. Shelton was still pulling the trigger over and over again long after he fired all the cartridges into the now lifeless body.

Shelton didn't struggle when Ed Foley pulled him away from the cabin to safety and sat him down on the grass, where he wept and then let out the horrific scream that would have been heard all the way down to the river.

The men seemed unsure what to do and were in a state of panic as they looked around for a sign that the kidnappers were still close by. Then Foley ordered one of the men to soak himself in the nearby trough and directed two other men to force the door open.

Once the door was open Foley called over the man who was now drenched with water and pushed him inside to retrieve what was left of the body.

Some of the men were discussing the tragedy and concluded that the kidnappers must have started a slow burning fire and timed it so that Daniel couldn't be helped. Or perhaps it was intended to be a warning and Daniel hadn't been meant to die.

Ed Foley strode towards the men, anger and

disapproval showing on his face when he told the men to stop nattering and ordered them to stay with Shelton. Then he galloped off towards the bridge. He was soon back and when he dismounted he was clutching a folded piece of paper. He placed a comforting hand on the sobbing Shelton's shoulder.

'This was pinned to the bridge, Mr Shelton, and it's addressed to you.'

Shelton took the paper and just stared at it as though in a trance. It took several promptings by Foley before Shelton eventually read the short message through his tear-filled eyes. He now knew that Daniel's death had been planned and was not a miscalculation. The kidnappers had done it because he, Shelton, had tried to trick them and had got the marshal involved. They would be in touch and if he tried any more tricks or brought the law in again, then his granddaughter would have the same end as her brother.

Shelton was usually in total control of everything, but now he had almost lost the will to live, let alone organize anything. His men looked on, waiting for their instructions, but none came until Ed Foley took over. He told some of the men to use their bedrolls that were tied to their saddles to cover Daniel Shelton's remains, which were chained to the chair that had been recovered from the cabin. He dispatched one man to ride into Craigy Plains and fetch the undertaker to make arrangements to take the body away. Foley would wait a short while, leaving Conrad Shelton with his grief before he would take him home. He would make certain that he was the one to break the news to Stephanie Shelton because she would need comforting. She would need to be hugged and that would be a pleasure he would look forward to. So far his plan was working just as he'd hoped. The next time Shelton wouldn't be stupid enough to try and trick him. He'd just been taught a lesson that he would never forget. Foley was feeling pleased with himself because he had just killed two birds with one stone and his cheating wife would soon be very lonely. Now he just needed to get rid of his other accomplices and he wouldn't have to share the ransom money.

TWELVE

The sky was dark and a fierce wind blew. The entourage attending Daniel's funeral was forced to hold on to their hats as they make their way from the white wooden church to the large cemetery just outside town. The plumes strapped to the heads of the magnificent team of white horses pulling the coffin carriage fluttered, but the animals were not perturbed by the extreme weather conditions.

The Craigy Plains cemetery was much larger than those in most towns with a similar population because the town and the nearby area lost half its residents during the fever outbreak, among them Conrad Shelton's wife. Conrad Shelton had reserved a special section of the cemetery and that's where the crowd had gathered to see Daniel's coffin lowered into the freshly dug grave beside that of his grandmother.

Men from the ranch stood back from the grave and the surrounding area that was occupied by Conrad and Stephanie Shelton, Mark Franklyn, Ed Foley, members of the town council and the Reverend Ian Markham.

Stephanie Shelton's face was pale and appeared almost white against the contrast of her long black coat. Her hair was pinned back and the wide-brimmed hat held in place with a black silk ribbon.

Conrad was dressed in the most expensive suit that money could buy, but his wealth couldn't bring him any comfort today and he struggled to maintain a brave face as the minister read out a tribute to his grandson. It described Daniel as a mixture of a brave soldier and a brilliant scholar even though he would never have been either.

Marshal Waters had visited the ranch on the day before the funeral to offer his condolences and ask how the 'accident' to Daniel had happened, but he was barred from entering the area of the ranch house. Ed Foley told him that Conrad Shelton didn't want him to set foot on the ranch ever again and neither he nor Ross would be welcome at his son's funeral. The marshal didn't know what he was supposed to have done, but he knew that feelings must be raw at this time and decided he would wait a while before he tried to find out what was going on at the Sheltons'. He knew from his last visit to the ranch that Conrad was hiding something and he hoped his silence hadn't cost him his grandson's life.

By the time the Shelton family left town the wind hadn't eased. Marshal Waters was looking through his office window when he spotted some of the black-suited ranch hands being parted from their hats as they were about to enter the saloon.

The marshal turned to Ross and said, 'It looks as if the

boys from the Shelton spread are going to pay their respects to young Daniel by drowning themselves in liquor. Foley is with them. I just don't trust that man.'

Ross had finished cleaning his gun and he joined the marshal at the window. 'He's always struck me as a friendly enough feller, so what makes you distrust him?' he asked.

'No real reason, except a hunch. That's one thing you learn being a lawman. You get to feel uneasy about certain people and you are always on your guard when they're around. I don't know how many times over the years that a hunch, or my intuition, has saved my life. The problem is that it's not a thing you can teach. I suppose it's a bit like Lon said about a fast draw being down to a natural gift. I hope you have a talent for both, young feller, and then you'll live to grow old, just like me.'

'To tell you the truth, Marshal, I don't think I want to grow old,' Ross replied.

Marshal Waters laughed. 'You will, son. Only the young don't want to grow old. You take my word, you will, especially if you end up with a lovely young woman like Stephanie Shelton. That's if that city dude, Franklyn, doesn't beat you to it.'

Ross sighed at the thought and told the marshal that there was never any chance of him getting back together with Stephanie while her grandpa was alive.

'I guess you're right. Conrad doesn't hide the fact that he hates your guts. Never mind, this town has it fair share of fine-looking young women. If I was a young man and free I wouldn't be looking further than Marielou, the singer over at the saloon. Now she's a real beauty and she's not like the other girls. I would say that she was brought up as a good churchgoing girl.'

'Talking of the saloon, Marshal, I think it's time I did my rounds.'

Marshal Waters lifted his watch out of his waistcoat pocket and said that he had some paperwork to do; he would join him later.

When Ross had gone the marshal did some serious thinking about recent events. He was certain that Daniel's death and the gruesome hangings were somehow linked and he was determined to find out what it was, whether Conrad Shelton liked it not. Shelton might be one of the richest men in the state, but that didn't give him more rights than the next man. The law was there to be obeyed by everyone unless they had a damned good reason for bending it, as the marshal had from time to time, but it had never been for his own gain.

THIRTEEN

Sloan had been watching the saloon door for the last hour. The woman they called Lisa had said that the man he was looking for would have been here half an hour ago. He sipped his beer. He would wait here all night if he had to. He'd learned to be patient in his line of work. Sloan had been christened Jeremiah Eli Sloan, but he'd given a good beating to any boys whom he'd grown up with who called him anything but Sloan, and now folks didn't know his real names.

One of the men sitting at the table near the bar asked him to join in a game of cards, but he just ignored him. He was used to people trying to creep around him, pretending to be friendly when they were just plain scared of him. He didn't like creeps. He didn't like the man who had hired him either, but he paid well, not that he needed the money. He didn't do what he did for money. He did it because it gave him a lift like no drink or the satisfaction from a horny woman could ever give. He often mused how his cruel pa and brother had teased him for being squeamish when they were killing chickens, or any of the animals they bred on their tiny homestead in Timberlake Ridge, a small town in western Arizona. Well, their teasing days were over because he had gunned them both down when he paid them a surprise visit just last fall. He had gone home expecting to get a big welcome now that he was famous, but they just laughed in his face and then called him a liar when he told them he was the famous and feared gunfighter. They'd heard of Sloan, but he was no weepy softie like he was. They called him weepy because he had cried at his dear ma's graveside. According to his pa it just wasn't natural for a real man to shed tears and he said that he was an embarrassment to the family name. Sloan hoped his ma would be proud of him because he always gave a man a fair chance. He was no backshooter, like some. He didn't have to be, because he reckoned he could outdraw any living soul. Some opponents gave him more pleasure than others and he was a mite disappointed that the man he was waiting for was going to be just too damned easy.

Ross had made the journey out to see Lon Vickery alone because the marshal had a meeting with the town council. Some of them had objected to Ross's appointment because they felt he wasn't the sort of man they wanted. Doc Hannington was likely the only one who would support the appointment so, unless the marshal did some persuasive talking, Ross might be hanging up his gun before the day was out. He'd had some long chats with the marshal and he was warming to the idea of staying in the job, so he would be disappointed if things didn't work out.

The trip to Lon Vickery's took Ross close to the small

ranch that he'd been struggling with against the cruel hand that nature had delivered to this part of the world. The cracks in the earth served as a reminder that come tomorrow he would be moving on if his badge was taken from him. If he had one reservation about his new job it was that it seemed mostly quiet, especially in the saloon. Now he had to break up fights instead of swapping punches and there wasn't much fun in that.

Lon had got him to try another gun from his large collection, but it didn't have the same feel as the old one and although Lon thought it had a smoother mechanism he advised Ross to stick with the one he felt most comfortable with. Lon wasn't the bragging sort, but Ross managed to get him to recall the time he'd had a shootout with the three Carter brothers in Sholan Creek.

'A lot of folks talk about that as if it was something special, but it wasn't. Jed Carter was pretty handy with a gun, but his brothers were just plain average. I probably owe my life to a dog.'

Ross looked down at Lon's devoted dog, Boy. Lon must have sensed it because he told him it happened long before he got Boy and the dog in Sholan Creek was just a stray.

'I didn't really want to take them on, but Jed was hell-bent on trying to kill me. He said that he'd heard that I'd gunned down two men who'd called me out and said if I was that good then why not try and take him and his brothers on. Someone had already run off to get the marshal to stop it, but the chicken-livered excuse for a man never came out of his office until the shooting had stopped.'

Ross was intrigued now and asked where the dog came into it.

'Well, you might think it's a bit of a tall story, but I swear it's true. My eyes had started to get worse and so when I stepped out on to Main Street to face the Carters I was thinking my time was up. Jed told me to make the first move, and I did. My first shot didn't get Jed plumb between the eyes, but he'd fired his last shot. I hit one of the other brothers in the chest, but I reckon the third one would have got me if a stray dog hadn't gone barking at his heels and distracted him.'

Ross shook his head and then patted Boy in a kind of reflex action. Lon told him that it wasn't the first time that a man had lost his life in a shootout because he had allowed himself to be distracted at a critical time.

Ross was anxious to know whether he was still a deputy, but his intention to go straight to the marshal's office to find out after returning to town was interrupted by a shout from across the street. He didn't know who the caller was, but whoever it was said that he was to go and see Doc Hannington straight away. Ross dismounted, tied his horse's reins to the hitch rail outside the office and then hurried towards Doc's surgery across the street. He couldn't think why the doc would want to see him as a matter of urgency, but the grim look on the doc's face told him that it wasn't about anything pleasant.

'Best come through, son. He's been asking for you. He's been hanging on, but he's getting weaker.'

Ross hadn't had time to prepare himself for what he was about to see. The marshal was lying on the bed; his face was a deathly white. His shirt had been ripped open and there was a blood-sodden dressing strapped across his chest. Waters managed a faint smile and when he spoke his voice was weak, almost a whisper. Ross swallowed hard to keep his emotion in check as he leaned closer so that he could hear.

'Listen, son,' said the marshal, then paused and gasped before he continued, 'don't take on that feller who did this to me. You're not ready for him just yet. You will be one day and you'll be a fine lawman. Promise me you'll let it be, because it just isn't worth risking your life. Someone will come along and get the better of him one day, they usually do.'

Before Ross could reply the marshal's eyes closed and he never spoke another word. Ross looked helpless and turned to Doc Hannington who moved in and checked the marshal's pulse.

'He's gone, son. It's a crying shame, but the town's lost a great servant and his killer is probably still in the saloon with a smirk on his face.'

'How did it happen, Doc?' Ross asked, the anger showing in his voice.

'The feller who came to get me said that a gunfighter who goes by the name of Sloan started slapping one of the girls about in front of the marshal and he goaded him to try and arrest him. When the marshal went for his pistol Sloan was quicker on the draw. That's how it happened, but according to some Sloan was waiting for the marshal. It was as though he was hell-bent on killing him, but why? What are you going to do, son? I couldn't hear everything the marshal said to you, but he seemed to want you to promise not to take Sloan on.'

'He did, but I never did get to promise the marshal that I wouldn't. The marshal was a fine judge of things and he probably meant I should live to fight another day. Perhaps I'll just bide my time. I assume from what the marshal indicated that I still have a job after today's council meeting?'

Doc Hannington smiled ruefully and said, 'I guess you do, son, but only because the marshal threatened to resign if they didn't let him keep you on. Who knows what will happen now that my dear friend is no longer with us? It's a crying shame because if ever a man earned the right to a long and peaceful retirement then George did.'

Ross thought the doc was a bit muddled until he explained that the marshal's real name was George Waters, but he never liked it and had begged his folks to call him Ron instead, so that was how he became known as Marshal Ron Waters.

Ross left the doc's surgery undecided whether to cross the street to the marshal's office, or head for the saloon and face the marshal's killer. It was something that Lon Vickery had mentioned earlier that day that made him decide that it was to be the saloon.

The Elm House wasn't too busy, but what little noise there was, stopped when he let the swing doors close behind him. Not all of the heads turned in his direction, but he was certain that all of the eyes did. The barman gestured with a sideways glance to point out where Sloan was sitting, but he had no need to do so because Sloan stood up and faced Ross.

'How's the old marshal, Deputy?' Sloan asked with a sneer.

'The marshal's dead. He died just five minutes ago.'

'Well, that's a real shame, because he was a brave man even though he was an old dumb ass. You would have thought that an old-timer like him would have known better than to pull a gun on me just because I gave one of the saloon whores a slap for making a crude suggestion to me. She isn't exactly what you'd call innocent, but more of a cheap slut, like the rest of the painted bitches in this dump.'

'That's not the way I heard it, you little squint-eyed piece of shit,' said Ross in a firm voice.

'Well, well. Maybe you're going to try to arrest me. Perhaps you are going to try to pull that old-fashioned pistol out faster than the marshal did. You must think that you are pretty handy to start throwing insults at a visitor to your pox-ridden town.'

'I hadn't ever worn a pistol until five days ago, so I could hardly claim to be handy, and I have never drawn against any man,' Ross explained.

'Is that so? Then you ought to watch your mouth, deputy boy, unless you've got some sort of death wish.'

'When I see shit I'll call it shit and that's what you are. I believe you go by the name of Sloan. You're the guy who has built a reputation on gunning down drunks who could hardly stand up, or young boys who couldn't hold their liquor and now you've sunk so low that you gunned down an old marshal who was about to retire. You really are shit.'

Sloan's face reddened and he scowled when some of men sitting at the card-table laughed. No one had laughed at him for a long time and this greenhorn deputy was to blame.

'Why aren't you going to arrest me, Deputy? Is it because you are yeller?' Sloan asked trying to recover his composure without any success.

'I just don't want you stinking out my nice clean cell. You do know that you smell like a giant piece of horseshit. I'm surprised any of the girls got within smelling distance of you.'

Sloan went for his gun. He had never drawn when he was angry and maybe that was why he ended up with a bullet between his eyes and a surprised expression on his dead face.

Some of those who had withdrawn from the line of fire looked at Ross in awe, others with disbelief. Ross calmly holstered his pistol. Before he strolled out of the saloon he said he was going to make arrangements to have Sloan buried in a spot that was reserved for the no-goods. Lon Vickery's advice about riling your opponent or making them feel overconfident had worked, or maybe it really was true that Ross had a God-given gift and a hand-speed that was a match for any man.

FOURTEEN

Marshal Waters's funeral had been held at noon and the saloon and shops had closed in honour of him. Ross had never seen so many people gathered in one place to pay their respects. He had been surprised that there was no representative from the Shelton family, but perhaps they were still doing their own grieving. The minister had made a very moving tribute to the marshal and for many it was the end of an era.

Ross had shaken Doc Hannington's hand afterwards. The doc, who had seen more tragedy than any other man in the town, had a tear in his eye. The marshal had no family, but Ross had made arrangement to bring Lon Vickery into town and have him taken home afterwards. He expected that a lot of men would be missing the marshal and perhaps none more than Lon, even though their meetings had not always been frequent. Lon had been making a gift for the marshal and had only just finished it the day he heard the marshal had been killed. It was a woodcarving of a marshal's badge and he'd been pleased when Ross had suggested that it be laid on the marshal's grave.

Ross took Lon back to the marshal's office after the funeral and was entertained by some of the old tales involving the marshal. Lon recounted the time when the marshal suspected a gang of newcomers of planning to rob the bank. While the men were in the bank he cut the straps holding their horse's saddles in place and when the men tried to ride off they fell off their horses as the saddles slipped. The men had gone into the bank to conduct legitimate business. The men were furious and Marshal Waters had a bright red face. Ross was still laughing at the story when Lon tensed and his hand moved towards his pistol. A few seconds later the office door opened and in trooped a deputation from the town council. They had all been at the funeral and the three faces wore solemn looks. Doc Hannington wasn't with them and Ross took that as a bad sign.

Mayor Peter Hoke, who owned the local livery and the Wyndham Hotel, was the chairman of the council. He had bushy ginger eyebrows, a small beard and clumps of hair on his cheeks. He was stocky in build and shorter than most men. He was regarded as something of an eccentric who still liked to work at the livery when he had no need to and would often recite passages from the Bible while grooming a horse. Some folks thought this practice was odd, while others believed that it had a soothing effect on the animals. Charles Pearson, the local bank manager, was dressed in his usual black suit. His thick gold-rimmed spectacles made his unusually large, piercing blue eyes look as though they belonged on a fish. He was a tall, almost gaunt man, and he tended to look on the serious side of life, especially when people wanted to borrow money from his bank. The third member of the trio was George Gilmore, who owned the town's newspaper, a happy-go-lucky man. His rotund frame was a testimony to his liking for food, mostly apple pie and anything that was sweet. The chubby face was always a healthy pink, even after his frequent long sessions in the saloon.

Mayor Hoke cleared his throat before he addressed Ross in a formal manner and started explaining that they were here on official business. Ross interrupted him and introduced Lon Vickery as a very good friend of the late marshal who had been a great help to him since he'd become a deputy.

The three men shook hands with Lon and they showed some signs of embarrassment for their bad manners. Then Mayor Hoke repeated his introduction and told Ross that a new marshal would be appointed later today.

Lon Vickery smiled in anticipation of Ross's promotion, but he soon discovered that he was wrong to do so when Hoke continued:

'There are a few preliminaries to be sorted out and the appointment will only be temporary. We have Mr Shelton to thank because he has offered to let Ed Foley fill the post and he has insisted that you stay on as his deputy.'

Ross was a modest man, but he had been thinking like Lon and had expected to be offered the post even though he was inexperienced.

Mayor Hoke seemed a mite embarrassed and he quickly concluded their business. The three left leaving Ross bemused and surprised, because as far as he knew Ed Foley had never been a lawman.

Lon waited for the door to close before he shook his head and said, 'Marshal Waters will just have turned over in his grave. He never did like Foley and he was a fine judge of men. I tell you, son, there's something fishy going on and you'd better be careful.'

'At least Foley will be able to keep the Shelton boys in check,' said Ross, who was still recovering from the surprise announcement. 'I wonder if he'll still spend so much time upstairs in the saloon while his wife is stuck in their cabin on the Shelton land.'

Lon didn't comment on Foley's womanizing and asked Ross if he thought he would be able to work with Foley.

'I might give it a go, mainly because in a funny sort of way I think I owe it to Marshal Waters, but I know what you mean about him turning in his grave. He made it clear to me that he didn't like Foley. Anyway, Lon, if you're ready then I think we should mosey over to the saloon and arrange for someone to take you home. I'd better hang around here in case my new boss turns up.'

Lon thanked Ross again for making arrangements for him to attend the funeral and gave him some more words of advice about Foley before he headed for home.

Ross returned to his office after seeing off Lon. He was trying to take everything in when he had a welcome visitor. It was Doc Hannington.

'I watched the three wise men leaving,' said the doc with a note of sarcasm in his voice. Then he asked Ross what he thought about Foley's appointment as marshal.

'I was surprised, Doc, but he has a lot of experience with handling men and he's tough enough for the job. He won't stand any nonsense from unruly cowboys. Marshal

Waters told me that he was the town's fifth marshal and the other four came to a violent end. Just like he did. So, it isn't exactly a desirable occupation that Foley is taking on, although I was told it was only temporary.'

'The marshal had high hopes for you, son, and I think a few of the troublemakers will be moving on after what you did to that feller who killed the marshal. Word will get out that you got the better of Sloan, who had a mean reputation, and it might act as a deterrent. I take it you will stay on as a deputy?'

'I'll give it a go because I don't have many options unless I move on. I've been wondering about Sloan since I had a talk with Dooley, the barman at the saloon, and he told me that he was surprised that Sloan goaded the marshal the way he did. It seems that Sloan was proud of his reputation of taking on all comers. Gunning down an old marshal wouldn't have got him much credit.'

The doc looked troubled before he spoke. 'I've been pondering whether I should tell you this, Steve, because it might not mean much. . . .'

'If it's got anything to do with the marshal's death, Doc, then I want to know what it is.'

The doc took a deep breath before he continued. 'Well, it's about Ed Foley, but it might be nothing to worry about.'

Ross was thinking about what the marshal had recently said about not trusting Foley.

'Let's hear it, Doc, because I have a feeling that it's kind of important.'

'Well, yesterday morning as I was on my way back to my surgery I looked down the gap between the Craigy Plains bank and Norman Monckton's store. I don't know what made me look because there's usually nothing there, except maybe some old boxes and packaging that Norman stores there. I saw Ed Foley talking to a man I didn't know. They were laughing and I didn't think anything of it.'

'So where's the harm in that, Doc? Perhaps it was just one of the men from the Shelton spread.'

'That's what I thought, until I saw this man again when I was called over to the saloon. You were there at the time and I pronounced him dead. The man was Sloan.'

Ross wasn't exactly surprised at what he'd just heard. He explained his thinking to the doc.

'It looks as though the marshal's intuition about Foley being someone to watch out for was right and Foley hired the services of Sloan to kill the marshal. The question is why, Doc?'

'Your guess is as good as mine, but the real question now is, will he try and get rid of you, the way he did the marshal. Whatever Foley does, you can bet he's doing it for Conrad Shelton. Maybe next time they won't risk a face-to-face and you'll be shot in the back.'

Ross was thinking hard. All his thoughts were on Conrad Shelton and he shared them once again with the doc.

'Doc, there's something going on at the Shelton place. Conrad Shelton acted real funny with the marshal and we didn't know why.'

'It seems that way, Steve, and I'm glad I told you. Now I'd best be getting back to my surgery. You take care, son, and watch your back. Just because Foley is the marshal doesn't mean that you will be safe from anything nasty that

Conrad Shelton might have planned for you.'

The doc paused at the door and had some parting words.

'There is something else that's been bothering me about that feller Mark Franklyn, but it isn't exactly serious. I hear that he's planning to marry Stephanie Shelton, but I was having a late card-game in the saloon the other night with my usual group and I saw Franklyn trying to sneak out. He'd obviously been upstairs with one of the girls, so perhaps our lawyer friend isn't quite the decent man he appeared to be.'

Ross joked that perhaps Franklyn had been giving the girl some legal advice, but the doc didn't seemed amused when he answered, 'I'd hate to see a nice young woman get lumbered with a womanizer, and I know you are fond of her as well.'

'I am, Doc, but I'm not her keeper and she's made her choice. I am surprised to hear what you said about Franklyn, because he just didn't seem the type to go with a saloon girl.'

Ross thanked the doc for warning him about Foley. He was already thinking that Conrad Shelton's change in attitude to Marshal Waters was somehow linked to the gruesome end of the two Brock brothers and young Tim Aitkin. He smiled at the thought that perhaps it was just a hunch, then his face filled with sadness. He was going to miss the old marshal more than he could ever have imagined. He vowed that he would find out whether Conrad Shelton or Foley had had anything to do with Marshal Walters's killing.

*

The meeting with the newly sworn-in Marshal Ed Foley later in the day didn't go quite as Ross had expected and it was a formal affair. After Foley had finished laying down how he intended to run things he asked Ross whether he would be staying on because if not he wanted to appoint a new deputy as soon as possible.

'Considering I was told you asked for me to stay on, Marshal, you're not exactly encouraging me with that long list of dos and don'ts you've just issued me with.'

Foley didn't show any reaction to Ross's comments. He just said that he had always been a believer in letting people who worked for him be in no doubt where they stood.

'Well, I think you've made it very clear, Marshal. To be honest, I was thinking of moving on anyway. I'll keep my land and perhaps come back when the drought ends and give it another go. So you go ahead and pick your own man.'

Again, Foley's face didn't show any reaction or surprise when Ross started to unpin his deputy's badge.

'I think you're doing the right thing, Ross. There's a big wide world out there for a young feller like you and there are more and better-looking women than you'll see in Craigy Plains. I wouldn't be hanging around here if I was your age.'

Ross felt good about his decision to move on, but Foley hadn't quite finished.

'But I'd like you to do me a favour and stay on for just a few days. I'm heading out of town in a couple of hours on some ranching business and might be away for a few days. I'll make it worth your while. Will you do that for me?'

Ross readily agreed, because he could do with all the money he could lay his hands in case he had trouble finding general farming, or ranching work. Foley thanked him and then hurried away to get ready for his trip. He didn't say where he going, and was a bit vague about when he was coming back.

FIFTEEN

Ed Foley liked the idea of being marshal and wearing his shiny new badge. He was thinking that the next time he visited the saloon Lisa would likely offer him special rates if he wanted to take one of the girls upstairs, but soon he would be able to afford anything he wanted. He would make the best of the job even though it wouldn't be for long. If everything worked out as he'd planned his days of taking orders would soon be over. He'd worked for slave-driver Shelton for over twenty years and done his dirty work for him and now it was time for him to take his reward. He was entitled to it, or so he had convinced himself. He and Shelton had every reason to be concerned if Mickey Brock was roaming free, ready to pop up and spill the beans as to how his brothers had died. Foley had cursed himself for leaving Mickey to that chicken-livered partner of his to finish the job off instead of doing it himself, as he had the other two. Joey had had a bull neck and it had been hard work removing his head even with the sharp hunting-knife. So when it came to Mickey he'd been just too tired to hack into another neck.

He should never have trusted a man whose hands had never seen a hard day's work. He'd had his doubts about him being able to do it, but he'd convinced Foley that he could, so he'd left him to it and gone to join the other men at the saloon.

There was always the chance that Mickey had been dragged away by some animal, but that was unlikely. Foley had only dug two holes so there could only be one explanation and that was that that dumb ass kid Aitkin had gone back to the scene for some reason and Mickey Brock had murdered him and planted his head so no one would come looking for him, Mickey. Well, Foley had other ideas and that was why he planned to take off after Brock. Now that he was marshal he could stop Ross poking his nose into what had happened, but he couldn't risk Mickey Brock just turning up in town. Foley would bring his head back to prove to Shelton that the danger was over and then he would take his own revenge on Mr Conrad Shelton. He also had some plans for the lovely young Stephanie. Foley had watched her blossom from a snooty little girl into the stunning woman she was today. He had seen the way she looked at the cowhands and reckoned that she needed a man who could give her more than that weedy city dude, Franklyn could. He had more than a hunch that she liked a man to be a man and perhaps the rougher the better and that's why she'd been sweet on Steve Ross, but Shelton had put a stop to that. He had a few chats with her recently and he could tell that she was a naturally horny woman who was being suppressed. He had already made plans for him and Stephanie, but first he had to make certain that nothing spoilt them.

Mary Foley watched her husband carefully place a spare shirt in his bedroll and gather his razor and few other belongings that he usually took on a cattle drive. She'd asked why he was going away and he said it was on a special job for Mr Shelton and everyone had been told to stay close to the ranch, but they hadn't been told why. So, what was her husband going to do that was making him fuss over his appearance like he was now and carefully brushing his light brown hair? He was still a good-looking man even with the start of a paunch. She knew that he spent time with the saloon girls, but she'd given up accusing him when he came home smelling of their cheap perfume and turning his back on her when she cuddled up to him wanting him to make love to her. He'd been acting strange the last few days; he'd been talking in his sleep calling out the name Stephanie over and over. Surely he couldn't be thinking of that sweet young Shelton girl who was young enough to be his daughter. It could only mean that there was a saloon girl who had the same name, but nothing would surprise her about her husband. Perhaps it was just as well that they had never been blessed with children and that was something else he blamed her for, even though it probably wasn't her fault because she had given birth after being raped as a young girl. The baby had died when it was a few weeks old and it had been years before she had met Foley and a long way from here. During the early days of their marriage she had wanted to tell him about the secret that she was carrying, but never did. She had also thought about mentioning her suspicions about him seeing saloon girls and neglecting her, but she would only end up with black eyes, or something more serious when he beat her. She gave a smile when he rode off because she wouldn't be missing him.

Maybe Jim Tully would come calling later if he knew that Foley was away unless he was going with him. When Jim had snuggled beside her in her bed last week while Foley was on one of his special trips, he had told her that he would take her away soon. She wondered what Foley would do if he found out that Jim Tully, who was the nearest thing he had to a friend had been keeping his side of the bed warm while he was absent. She didn't really believe Tully's promise to take her away, but she was happy to see him because she had needs that he could satisfy and make her life that much more bearable.

SIXTEEN

Lisa smiled when the two fresh faced kids strutted up to the bar. She would bet her last dollar that neither of them had ever been with a woman, or maybe even kissed a girl. She had lost count of the number of 'first timers' that she'd helped experience the thrills of being with a woman and some of them had given her more pleasure than she received from some experienced men. The slightly built one with the tousled fair hair ordered two beers while the stocky one with the dark curls looked around the bar as though he was either looking for someone, or weighing up the opposition. Curly, as she had already labelled him, was wearing two low slung pistols, but Shyboy had just the one.

She smiled at them when they took their first gulp of beer and then looked in her direction. Curly remained stone-faced while his buddy gave her a shy smile and his face turned pink. If she had a choice she would pick the shy one and let one of the younger girls have the other one who seemed determined to project how tough he was. She just hoped he wouldn't spit on the floor the way some men did as if to prove how tough they were.

Cameron Dyke scanned the bar and kept his voice low when he said, 'Hey, Frankie, that old hag at the end of the bar keeps looking this way. I think she wants to do some business with one, or perhaps both of us.'

Frankie Crowe looked in Lisa's direction. He then quickly turned back again, but his face went pink. 'She's just trying to be friendly. Anyway, she's old enough to be our grandma.'

'My pa told me that all women are young and beautiful if you drink enough beer,' Cameron said. Then he added some more of his pa's wisdom. 'The secret is not to overdo it, otherwise you end up wasting your money.'

'You don't want to drink too much. Remember what you came here to do and it wasn't to fool around with any saloon girls,' Frankie cautioned.

Cameron took a gulp of beer. Then he said, in an even lower voice, 'I'm still not sure about this, Frankie. My pa said he'd seen Sloan in action over in some mining town just last year. I can't remember the name of the place, but Pa said he was something really special.'

'And you're something really special, Cameron. They said that feller you gunned down last week in Mooresville was damned good as well, but he never even got his gun fully out of the holster before you plugged him. I can still see that funny look on his face before he crashed to the floor.'

Frankie laughed at the memory. Cameron smiled, then said, 'He shouldn't have tried to muscle in on that saloon girl who was talking to me. Now *she* was special, not like Grandma Hag over there. Hang on, she's coming over to us.'

Lisa gave them her best smile as she stood close to them at the bar. She introduced herself and asked them if they were looking for a good time.

Frankie was taken back when Cameron replied, 'You bet we are, honey, and you look the sort of woman that we'd want to have it with. We've got to take care of something first, but then we'll come and find you.'

Lisa was surprised by his comments. He was a cocky little feller and maybe he wouldn't be a first timer, but she was still convinced that the blushing boy, who was gawping down her blouse, had never seen a naked woman. If she stayed any longer she would have to tell him to put his tongue back in. She told them she would look forward to seeing them later, winked at them and wiggled her way back to her favourite spot.

When Lisa was out of earshot Frankie nudged Cameron and said, 'I thought you didn't like her. Do you think we'll have enough to pay her?'

'You are dumb sometimes, buddy. I just told her that so she would leave us alone. Let's have another beer and leave. I'm feeling a bit horny after talking to her about it, so perhaps we can see if there's another saloon in town, or maybe there might be a barn dance, or something and we can pick up a couple of local girls.'

'But that's not what we came here for. If you can beat this feller, like I know you can, then you'll be famous and you'll be able to have your pick of saloon girls.'

'I've changed my mind, Frankie. I ain't scared or anything, but I just don't feel in the mood.'

Frankie looked over Cameron's shoulder, then turned and looked down at his near-empty glass of beer. 'That's a pity,' he said, 'because he's just walked in.'

Cameron swirled round, expecting to find that it was his buddy's idea of a joke, but it wasn't. Steve Ross was looking in their direction.

'Hey, Deputy,' Cameron called out to Ross, who had joined Lisa at the other end of the bar.

'What's troubling you, kid?' Ross replied. He stepped away from Lisa and added, 'You sound sort of nervous. Is everything all right?'

'I ain't nervous. I want to know if you are the son of a bitch that gunned down my pa in this very saloon. His name was Sloan.'

Frankie was thinking that his buddy was one heck of a convincing liar, pretending to be Sloan's son.

'I didn't know that Sloan had any kinfolk, kid, but I am the one who killed him and I'm glad that I did. He was lower than a snake's belly and I'm thinking that you might just take after him. Now, why don't you and your buddy leave those drinks and get the hell out of here.'

Frankie was thinking that what the deputy had said about leaving now seemed like a good idea.

'Let's go, Cameron. I don't like the beer in here,' said Frankie. He started to move away from the bar.

'Stay put, Frankie. We can take this feller just like we planned. He looks pretty ordinary to me.'

Cameron put on his meanest look. 'We ain't leaving here, Deputy,' he said defiantly, 'and I don't think you're good enough to take the two of us. But if you're feeling lucky, why don't you try?'

'You're getting yourself all confused, kid. I thought you'd come here to settle a score over your no-good pa.

So, whenever you and your chicken-livered buddy feel like making a move on me, I'm ready. It's your call, but you can still walk away.'

The men sitting at a table behind Ross and others behind Cameron and Frankie had been listening with interest to the exchange, but now there was a scuffling of chairs and they all retreated from the possible line of fire.

'Come on, Cameron, this feller has got a trick up his sleeve. Let's go,' Frankie urged once again.

Cameron moved his hands close to his pistols' handles, then muttered to Frankie in a low voice, 'When I say "now", let him have it.' He paused and then shouted, 'Now.'

Frankie's hand had reached his pistol and Cameron had almost cleared the holster with both his pistols when they realized that Ross's gun was pointing at them.

The deafening sound as Ross fired two shots had the youngsters holding up their hands in pathetic attempts to shield their faces. Ross had decided not to follow Lon's advice: to try and aim for between their eyes. He had deliberately aimed over their heads.

'Don't shoot us,' Cameron pleaded when he realized that they were still alive. They both raised their hands above their heads.

'Perhaps I ought to kill you both now, because I don't want you coming back for a rematch.'

'We won't,' said Frankie in a voice that had suddenly become boyish and pleading.

'Sloan wasn't my pa and, as Frankie said, we won't come back,' added Cameron in support.

Ross pretended that he wasn't convinced. He removed

100

their weapons and threw them to the floor. He pondered for a while before he said, 'Right, get out of here and out of town. If I ever see you again then I will shoot you on sight. I won't give you any warning because I will always have two bullets with your names on.'

Cameron and Frankie rushed from the saloon. They didn't hear Lisa say to herself, 'Deputy Ross, you just spoilt my little bit of pleasure I had lined up for later with one of those handsome boys.'

SEVENTEEN

Saturday was usually the busiest day of the week at the Elm House saloon, but tonight was extra busy because one of the Shelton crews had just returned from a long cattle drive, eager to quench their thirst and spend some of their pay on the saloon girls.

The Elm House had originally been owned by five brothers who came from England, Joe, William, Charlie, Ned and Cornelius Thomas. A sixth brother Jimmy had planned to come with them, but met up with a lady before they were due to sail and changed his mind. The brothers had moved on some years ago to try their luck at gold prospecting. The saloon had changed hands many times since, but always kept the original name. Cornelius Thomas had been a keen aboriculturist and had arranged for a small elm tree to be shipped from England. It had been planted at the rear of the saloon. Some say that it had been a favourite stopping point for the many stray dogs that wandered about the town and that that was the reason it had withered and died.

Conrad Shelton was a regular visitor to the Elm House, always on Saturdays. It was just before eight o'clock when he entered through the swing doors and made his way towards Lisa. Lisa turned away from the cowboy she had been talking to and gave Shelton the usual royal welcome.

'It's nice to see you again, Mr Shelton. Let's take a seat over there,' Lisa suggested. She led him towards one of the few quiet spots away from the bar.

The youngest of the newly arrived Shelton boys nodded in the direction of Shelton. He remarked with some surprise that it looked like Mr Shelton.

'That's our man. He's one of the regulars in here,' said Billy Boardman, then added with a knowing smile, 'Lisa must have a new girl lined up for him.'

'What, you mean he'll be going upstairs?' asked the newcomer in some disbelief that his esteemed new boss would even frequent the Elm House, let alone have himself a saloon girl.

'Well, he's not here for the beer,' Boardman replied. He and the other Shelton boys laughed.

'But he's an old grandpa. Surely he can't be doing – you know what?' the newcomer questioned.

'According to the girls' old man Shelton is a bit of legend when it comes to upstairs. I hear that some of the girls call him the Con the Stallion.'

'You're kidding me on. I bet he's just called in to discuss some business.'

'He certainly has, but it's upstairs business,' Boardman quipped, and there was more laughter.

'I thought he might be comforting poor Martha Aitkin tonight,' suggested one of the men.

'You mean the ma of that poor ranch hand who had that terrible death,' queried the newcomer.

'That's her. She works at the house and has a little cabin not far from it,' replied Boardman. 'Whenever Tim was out guarding the cattle at night old Conrad would always go calling on Martha. Some say they'd sit up all night discussing all manner of things, such as history and religion.'

'He must be a caring sort of man, Mr Shelton,' said the naïve newcomer.

'Oh, he cares for Martha,' said Boardman, then added sarcastically, 'Mr Shelton could have been a preacher.'

There were more bouts of laughter from the gathering, except the young newcomer who looked a bit bewildered.

Shelton and Lisa were in more serious mood than his men. He was seeking more reassurance from Lisa.

'And this girl is definitely special in the way that I like them and not like the other trollops you have working here?'

Lisa would have liked to tell him what a foul-mouthed old pig he was, but she was too dependent on his money, so she didn't.

'Oh, this one is really special. If anyone deserved to be described as pure as the driven snow then it's this girl. I promise you that you will not be disappointed with her.'

Billy Boardman watched as Conrad Shelton made his way upstairs without any trace of embarrassment. As was his usual practice, Shelton paused and looked around the bar as if to check that he had been seen.

Boardman nudged the newcomer and said, 'There he goes. I told you. Now if that piano feller stops playing and you listen very carefully you might hear the girl upstairs moaning and groaning when Conrad gets to work.'

The lad's mouth went dry at the mere thought, and one of the more serious members of the group remarked that he hoped he could perform like Conrad could if he ever got to reach his age.

Shelton walked along the upstairs corridor to the end room where Lisa had said the girl would be waiting. The room was dimly lit with candles and he could smell flowers, not the usual cheap perfume smell. He paused in the doorway and listened to the soothing, gentle sound of humming. He was usually abrupt with the girls, but when he looked at the young naked body stretched out on the bed he was shocked by her beauty. He figured that she could be no more than seventeen years old and her black hair was nestled on her shoulders. She was the first oriental girl he had ever seen in the flesh and he was thinking that there could be no one more beautiful in the whole world. She sat up and gave him a small bow as she clasped her hands together. He fixed his eyes on her firm young breasts, which were large for such a small-framed girl. Her lips were fleshy and moist, but she wore no make-up. He was mesmerized by her dark-brown eyes that revealed her shyness, but they were inviting. He asked her what her name was. She replied in a gentle, almost subservient way.

'I am May Ling and it will be my honour if I can bring you some pleasure, sir.'

She rose from the bed and bowed once more before she started to undress him. He wanted to stop her and explain that he had only come to talk with her and lie

105

beside her, but he seemed powerless to do so. She spoke words that flattered the firmness of his body even though it was fat and wrinkled. For a moment he almost believed her; then he pushed her away and said they should lie down. She nestled against him and kissed him on each cheek and, briefly, on his mouth. He groaned as the softness of her skin rubbed against him, willing him to become aroused, but even she would fail.

What followed was a familiar routine when Shelton visited a girl. He was left sweating and agitated, blaming the girl for not positioning herself right. On this occasion he accused her of being frigid.

'I'm sorry to disappoint you, sir,' she apologized, clearly upset that he was displeased.

Shelton didn't reply as he hurriedly dressed and told her to do the same. He instructed her to keep quiet while he settled in a nearby chair and poured himself a drink of his favourite whiskey, which had been left there by arrangement. Shelton consumed his third glass before he looked at his watch and decided it was time to leave.

Before he left he told the girl that she was not to breathe a word about what had happened, then he tossed her a number of dollar bills. May Ling was richer than she had ever been and she was still a virgin.

Shelton composed himself before he ventured down the stairs to the bar and made his way to the table where Lisa was sitting by herself. He stayed just long enough to say, 'She was useless. Make sure that she doesn't leave her room and is on the stagecoach out of here tomorrow.'

Shelton was smiling like a cat that had got the cream as

106

he passed his men at the bar, but once outside the saloon he scowled as he headed towards his waiting carriage, then barked out an order for the driver to take him home.

EIGHTEEN

Martha Aitkin's world seemed over and she wondered whether she would ever recover from the loss of her only child, especially because of the gruesome way her lovely boy had died. She might have coped had it been on the battlefield, or a tragic accident, but not after the way he had departed from this world.

Martha Aitkin had been brought to town on the wagon that made regular trips to pick up fresh supplies. She had spent an hour at her son's graveside, quietly talking to him and telling him how she had worshipped him and how proud she had been that he had become the man of the house when he'd started working.

Martha had trudged her weary way from the cemetery up Main Street. The visit to her son's grave had given her the resolve to carry out what she knew she had to do. When she'd reached Monckton's store she'd slumped on to the bench outside to gather her thoughts before she embarked on the first part of her plan.

Martha Aitkin was only forty-three years old and still attractive, but today her face carried the signs of her recent grieving and her blue eyes were bloodshot through weeping and lack of sleep. The blonde shoulder-length hair was straggly and greasy. The dress that she had been sleeping in these past days was crumpled and she wouldn't have looked out of place had she been carrying a begging-bowl. Martha had led a hard life, mostly as the result of living with a violent and drunken husband. She hadn't mourned his loss when he'd been shot on his way home from a night in the saloon just over three years ago. No one knew who had done it, but he had made more than a few enemies with his violent temper and foul mouth when he'd been drinking. Since shortly after his death she had been living with Tim in the small cabin on the Shelton ranch and she had been happy. She could have remarried one admirer, but didn't, partly because of her previous bad experiences, but mostly because of the special relationship she had with Conrad Shelton.

Martha had been told to take some time off from her duties at the Sheltons' to try to get over Tim's death, but she had decided to keep busy. Yesterday she overheard a conversation when she had delivered food to the bunkhouse that had left her full of hatred. Most of the cowhands had ridden off after they'd eaten, but Lee Shaw, who had been Tim's best friend, had stayed behind to clear out the barn. She confronted him about what she had overheard. He eventually gave in to her pleas to tell her the truth about the hangings. She heard how it had upset Tim and that some of the men thought that Tim might have gone back to the place where the men had been left, to give them a decent burial. It seemed that her sweet young son had died because of the cruel actions of two men. She would never forgive Conrad Shelton and Ed Foley.

Martha had barely acknowledged those who passed by on the sidewalk offering their condolences. She had been preoccupied with her thoughts and had counted the contents of her purse for the third time when she clipped it closed and made her way into Norman Monckton's store.

Norman Monckton told her how sorry he was to hear about Tim and asked her how she was coping. She thanked him for his kindness, but when he asked if he could help her he wasn't prepared for her reply.

'I want to know how much a pistol is, Mr Monckton.'

Monckton laughed away his surprise and asked, 'And what would you be wanting a pistol for, Martha?'

Martha had prepared her answer and it sounded convincing when she replied, 'I just don't feel safe after what happened to Tim, now that I'm living on my own, but I might not have enough money to buy one.'

Monckton gave her a sympathetic look. He said that he could understand, but he assured her that she was as safe as anyone could be because he'd heard that the Shelton ranch was like a fortress.

'I know I'm being silly, but my cabin isn't that close to the ranch house. I have never fired a pistol, but it would give me some comfort.'

Monckton liked Martha. She had been through hell, so he decided to help her.

'I understand, Martha. Now let's see how much money you have.'

Martha emptied the contents of her purse on to the

counter. He could see at a glance that she didn't have enough, but he was a soft-hearted man on these occasions and told her that she had more than enough for his cheapest model.

Martha Aitkin left the store with a pistol, six bullets and a dollar to spare, thanks to Monckton's benevolent gesture, but he was troubled. He hoped that he hadn't just made a big mistake as he remembered the widow Morrison, who had ended her lonely days with a bullet in her head just last fall.

NINETEEN

Ross was about to mount the steps of the Wyndham Hotel when the man he was hoping to see came down them from the main entrance. The hotel was the only one in town, but one of the finest in the territory. It discouraged rowdy cowboys from staying there mainly through the high tariff it charged. Ross had always been curious to see the inside, but for the moment his curiosity would have to wait.

'Howdy, Mark, I was hoping to have a talk. I came over to see you last night, but you had some company.'

Franklyn looked uncomfortable as he returned Ross's greetings. He said that he was in rather a hurry and had a meeting to attend at the Shelton ranch. He suggested that if Ross didn't mind walking with him to the livery they might talk as they went.

There was silence for a moment as they set off down Main Street. They made an unusual contrast with their very different attire. The silence was broken when they both started to talk at the same time. Ross laughed and suggested that Franklyn went first.

'I have been meaning to talk to you, Steve, but it's kind

112

of difficult. Did you see who I was with last night.'

'Only the back of her as she disappeared into the hotel,' Ross replied.

Franklyn gave a sigh, 'She's an old friend from Linton Town where my home is and she arrived unexpectedly,' he said. 'To be honest she's more than an old friend. We were planning to get married before I got the job of working for Conrad Shelton. When I got involved with Stephanie I wrote to her and called it off. I felt really bad about it, but now we plan to get together again.'

'Hmm, it sounds like you have a complicated love life, buddy.'

'Well, it looks as though everything might turn out for the best. You included.'

'I don't follow. Where do I come into this?' asked a puzzled Ross. He didn't really know much about Franklyn, but never figured him for the sort who would be involved with two women at the same time.

'Well, Stephanie seemed less than keen on the idea of us getting married and I'm certain that she still has strong feelings for you. I'm going to tell her about Robyn when I see her this morning and I think she's going to be relieved, although I don't expect her grandfather to be too pleased.' Franklyn paused, then changed the topic. 'Anyway, Steve, what was it that you were coming to see me about?'

Ross was still thinking about the implications of what Franklyn had said about Stephanie, but he answered the question.

'I was going to ask you if there was anything going on at the Shelton place that I should know about? When I visited there with Marshal Waters he seemed to think that the Sheltons were hiding something, and he wondered whether it was connected with that terrible thing that happened to Daniel.'

'There is something going on, Steve. I can't tell you too much, but it will be sorted soon. You will only make things worse if you try to get involved, but you have my word that nothing's going to happen to Stephanie, Conrad will make certain of that.'

They had reached the livery and shook hands before Ross turned away and headed back up Main Street. He would be sorry when Franklyn left town, but he had a lot of thinking to do about Stephanie. Perhaps recent events over her brother had made her see things differently and maybe she was ready to stand up to her grandfather.

Ross was still daydreaming when he reached the marshal's office, wondering how Stephanie would like the idea of being a marshal's wife. Hank Lewis was waiting outside and he looked troubled.

Lewis was Ross's nearest neighbour whose farm had been ruined by the drought, but he had been determined to hang on. Lewis was of medium height, but broader in the shoulder even than Ross and had the arms of a blacksmith. He looked older than his twenty-eight years, his blond hair was beginning to thin and he would be as bald as his late pa before too long. His face was drawn as he puffed nervously on the small cigar. Ross had never seen him smoke and figured it must be something he'd taken to since his troubles had worsened.

Ross asked what he was doing here because it didn't look as though it was a social call. When Lewis had finished explaining Ross's face had also taken on a worried look. He invited his neighbour into his office. When both men were seated Ross sighed heavily after he had pondered what Hank had asked him.

'I'm not sure if that's a good idea, Hank. I know times are hard, but being a deputy marshal isn't the job for a man with a wife and three young children. I was planning on moving out as soon as Ed Foley gets back and he'll only be doing the marshal's job on a temporary basis.'

'Steve, I wouldn't be asking if I wasn't desperate. I've reached the end of the road with the farm and I can't even afford to get us out of this town. I even had to sell my horse last week. I've walked in here to see you.'

Ross didn't deliberate too long because he could see how anxious and desperate Hank was.

'All right, Hank. We'll give it a try, but the pay isn't that good. I'll speak to the town council and tell them that you'll be able to take over my job. If they don't agree I'll tell them I'm resigning. I'll ask them about getting you a horse. At least you have your own gun, which is more than I had.'

Hank pumped Ross's hand and thanked him over and over again. Then he asked him how come he was so good with a gun if he'd never owned one before he became a deputy.

'Hank, if I told you how I learned to handle a gun you just wouldn't believe me, but I'd willingly pass on any tips that my tutor gave me. It wasn't Marshal Waters, but he did teach me lots of other things in the short time I worked for him. Now, let's go and see Peter Hoke about appointing you, at least until Foley gets back.'

115

*

The town council duly approved of Ross's new deputy. He didn't have to make any threats about resigning, which would have left the town without a lawman. They also provided Hank with a horse and gave him a small advance on his wages.

Ross had never been in charge of anyone before and when Hank reported for duty the following day he had to keep telling Hank to stop addressing him as 'Marshal'.

'You're making me feel old before my time, Hank. So call me Steve and that's an order. And remember I'm only sort of acting marshal while Foley's away.'

Ross spent some time going through the office paperwork. He was pleased when Hank told him that when he was a boy he had worked for a short while in a newspaper office, so he was used to filing and all that kind of stuff. After the office routine had been explained, including where the various keys were kept for the cells and gunracks Ross thought it was time to impart some practical advice.

'Most of what I am going to tell you, Hank, is what Marshal Waters told me. It all made good sense. He told me that any lawman had to show confidence when confronting a situation, especially when dealing with strangers. The ones that you least have to worry about are the mouthy ones who are trying to show everyone how tough they are. That sort is usually as weak as beer in some of the saloons we've all been in, although I am glad to say that our own Elm House is not amongst them.'

When Hank told him that he wasn't much of a judge of

people Ross assured him that it would come with experience. Then he continued, 'The ones to really worry about are the sly ones. Sloan didn't brag about how good he was, he just goaded people into going for their guns. At least you had a chance with him because he wasn't a backshooter.'

Hank looked troubled for a moment when he remembered what Ross had done to Sloan.

'I've never killed anyone, Steve, but I will if I have to. Was Sloan the first man that you killed?'

Ross told him that he'd killed once before Sloan, but he didn't go into the details except to say that it hadn't been with a gun.

'I think that's enough chinwagging for now, Hank, so why don't we mosey over to the saloon and let people get used to seeing that shiny new badge of yours. The saloon girls will do a bit of teasing, but you'll be able to handle them, you being a married man.'

TWENTY

Ross looked out of his office window again. He was restless. He had things on his mind. He was regretting sending Hank over to see Lon Vickery, because it might have helped to talk things through with him. Until a short time ago he'd had no worries apart from the drought. He was his own free spirit and ready to do a bit of travelling and live a little before he stopped fist-fighting and thought about settling down. Now he was the acting marshal and that meant responsibility. He had also been thinking about those kids in the saloon who had wanted to take him on with a gun. Lon Vickery had warned him that his reputation would spread when the word got around that he had gunned down Sloan, but he hadn't expected it to happen so quickly. The thing that was causing him most anxiety was Stephanie. His thoughts drifted back to their last meeting and the things she'd said and her feelings. The timing was all wrong for both of them, but he couldn't get her out of his mind.

Stephanie had come to see Ross the day after her

brother's funeral. She explained that she had made up her mind to accept Franklyn's proposal. Her grandfather had suffered enough with the death of her brother and she couldn't upset him by seeing Ross again. He wished she hadn't kissed him goodbye, so leaving him in no doubt about her true feelings for him. She said that she was going to stay with a friend for a few days before she told Franklyn about her decision. She'd run off with tears in her eyes. He'd wanted to go after her and beg her to come with him and start a new life away from her grandfather, but he didn't. He wondered what she would do now that Franklyn must have told her about his own intentions to get back with the woman who was in town. She would be confused and maybe waiting for Ross to do something.

He was on the point of deciding what to when his thoughts were interrupted.

'What the hell,' Ross muttered to himself when he saw the rider pull up his horse outside the marshal's office. He'd never seen a man covered in so much blood, but he seemed sprightly enough as he dismounted from the black stallion that was so familiar to Ross. Strapped to the saddle-bags were two makeshift sacks that looked as though they were made from bedrolls. The man had begun untying them.

Ross opened the office door as the man mounted the steps.

'I need to see the marshal,' he said. His voice sounded weak and on closer inspection the man looked as though he had been on a hunger strike. His face was gaunt and deathly white, except for splashes of blood, and his eyes were sunken.

119

'In case you haven't noticed, buddy, I am the marshal, or at least the acting marshal. The name's Steve Ross. You look as though you've been in a lot of trouble and you'll need to explain how you come by that stallion there, that belongs to Stephanie Shelton. Do you need to see the doc?'

'No, I need to see you, I suppose. What happened to Marshal Waters?'

Ross's face showed his sadness when he replied, 'I'm afraid the marshal's dead. Shot last week by some lowlife. What's your name, stranger?'

'I'm no stranger to this town, I'm Mickey Brock and I recognize you now. I saw you digging up those small graves last week. Two of those heads that you dug up belong to my brothers. The third one was some kid who came back for another look and I killed the curious little son of a bitch.'

'That was Tim Aitkin you killed, mister, and he was no more than a boy. Why the hell did you do that?' asked Ross, who had just lost any sympathy for this wretched-looking man who still hadn't explained how come he had Stephanie's horse. It had to be her horse because Ross was certain that there couldn't be another horse like it in the whole of Arizona.

'That kid was there when they strung up me and my brothers up and he came back for another look. He was a sick little bastard and that's why I killed him.'

Brock nodded at the blood-sodden bedrolls when he said, 'I killed those two as well, not more than a couple of hours ago. That's how I came by that fine horse outside and I've come to give myself up.'

120

Ross resisted the temptation to unwrap the bedrolls. He asked Brock to explain what had happened to his brothers. He waited until Brock had revealed everything about the gruesome events that had taken place, and he decided it was not surprising that Brock's face looked like that of a man who had been rescued after being buried alive.

Something didn't quite fit and Ross asked, 'Why didn't you die from the hanging just like your poor brothers? And how come Foley didn't brand you as well?'

Brock turned around and lifted the shirt that must have belonged to Tim Aitkin. Ross winced when he saw the brand mark on the fleshy part of Brock's left hand side.

'But surely you must have cried out when that happened. Why didn't you end up having your head hacked off?'

'I ain't a religious man, but someone must have been watching over me. I don't really have an answer except that I must have been unconscious when I was branded. I sure did feel it when I came to at the foot of that tree. I must have just dropped to the ground. I remember seeing this young fancy-dressed city-looking dude feller with a knife in his hand. I reckon I scared the shit out of him when I opened my eyes. That was the last thing I remembered. I'd never seen him before.'

'If it isn't a dumb question, why have you come here after all that you've been through?'

'I just want justice for my brothers and I want Shelton to suffer. I blame myself and that bitch, Stephanie Shelton.'

Ross was taken aback by the mention of Stephanie. He

asked why Stephanie was to blame.

'My brothers were right about her when they said that she was just a tease. She used to smile at me when we came into town. She was no better than those saloon girls. Sometimes I would ride on the Shelton land just to see her and she would give me one of those special smiles. I thought she liked me. No woman has ever smiled at me, at least not unless I paid her.'

'Stephanie Shelton's just a sort of friendly person who smiles at everyone,' said Ross, more by the way of trying to calm down Brock, who was becoming agitated, than to defend Stephanie's good name.

'Well, she wasn't very friendly when I saw her out riding on the day before my brothers ended up dead. She shouted at me and told me to stop pestering her. She called me something which I couldn't hear properly, but it sounded like, "you ugly little man". Then the next day the Shelton boys came and got me and my brothers and accused us of crazy things that weren't true. We never did write any letters and threaten to kidnap anyone. They wouldn't listen when we told them that none of us could read or write. Well, it's all different now and Miss High and Mighty Stephanie Shelton's smiling days are over.'

Ross peeled back the blanket and froze when he saw the first head. It wasn't like the others and although pale, it was otherwise unmarked and looked as though it was still alive. Ross's sympathy for Brock left him; he wanted to grab the sick, demented creature by his neck and beat the shit out of him. He was no better than those who were responsible for his brothers' deaths. Ross would be riding out to the Shelton ranch to deliver some very tragic news, but first he would see who the second head belonged to. Then he would lock up Mickey Brock.

TWENTY-ONE

Conrad Shelton took his third gulp of whiskey in as many minutes. He could hardly bear to look at the latest photograph of his granddaughter, which was on his desk, but he did. The tears welled in his eyes and then he sobbed. She reminded him once again of his dear wife. It was not a reminder of her beauty, but of the grief-stricken face she had shown in the days after they had buried their son and his wife. No brother and sister could have been closer than Stephanie and Daniel had been and now Daniel was gone. He stared at the saddle-bags of money and blamed himself for Daniel's terrifying death. Franklyn had made special arrangements with the bank to get the money, which had involved signing over the Shelton property. He had asked himself over and over again who could be behind this. It could only be Ed Foley and his accomplices. Stephanie had now gone missing and so had Foley. Ed Foley had known that Shelton wasn't going to pay the ransom on the day that he went to get Daniel and Foley was also the only man who knew about the Clarkson family. Shelton looked at his watch and tapped his fingers on the desk. He could hear some movement outside, but would not risk going to investigate. He would wait until the study door opened and hope that this would all end soon.

Shelton would leave the town when it was all over. At least Stephanie had Franklyn and he still hoped that she would come to her senses and marry him. All that nonsense she mentioned the other day about loving Ross was not herself talking. She was still in shock over the loss of her brother.

Shelton sighed. His eyes misted over again and his voice choked with emotion as he spoke to the photograph.

'There are things you don't know about me, honey. I have done things that I'm not proud of and maybe I deserve what's happened, but I did it for my family and now there's not going to be much left for you. I've let you down and that hurts me.'

The study door started to open, Shelton froze in anticipation of meeting the man he had just silently vowed he would have hunted down if it was the last thing he did. There would be no hiding place for the man who had caused him so much misery.

Shelton had remembered what a low regard Foley had for women and that had brought him fresh agony, wondering whether he had forced himself on Stephanie.

The man in the doorway had hatred in his eyes and he was pointing a gun at Shelton. It seemed that Foley hadn't the guts to face him and had sent an accomplice.

Shelton was tempted tell him that he would only hand the money to Foley, but he wouldn't risk antagonizing the man while Stephanie was in danger.

'Take your money and tell Foley that I'll find him if the last thing I do.'

'Don't you recognize me, Mr Shelton? You must remember me, although we have both changed. You look like a fat sweaty pig sitting there with your blotchy red face and bleary eyes and you stink even from this distance. You must remember the name Maben and all those threats you made against my pa. You haven't even used the land you stole from him. I remember you at my pa's funeral the day after he'd taken his own life and was found hanging in our barn. You came over to me and my ma and offered to help. I spat on your fine tailored suit. You must have remembered that. You offered us money, but Ma wouldn't take it. I came here for justice, but I'll be taking that money.'

Shelton's heart thumped in his chest, his mouth was dry and sweat had formed on his top lip. His forehead was wet with it.

Tommy Maben was enjoying seeing Shelton's panic and distress so much that he hadn't heard the movement behind him. When he did, and turned, it was too late. The bullet thundered into his chest. He pitched forward on to Shelton's desk, then fell to the floor. Tommy Maben would never get the revenge he came for, because he was dead.

Shelton's relief was mixed with surprise and the realization that he had completely misjudged the man who had just saved his life. That man, who had never worn a gun, had shown not the slightest hesitation in killing a man just a few feet from him. He would be proud to welcome this man into his family if he married his granddaughter.

'I owe you my life, son. That madman blamed me because his pa was a chicken-livered coward who took his own life.'

'That feller didn't come for your money. That was Foley's idea.'

'You mean Foley might still turn up? You'd better get out of here because if he finds you here who knows what he'll do to Stephanie.'

'Foley was never going to turn up here today,' explained Franklyn.

'I don't understand. What about the last ransom note? You saw it.'

'Oh, that was real enough, but Foley didn't send that one.'

Shelton noticed that Franklyn hadn't holstered his pistol after shooting Maben. Now it was pointing at him.

'It's you, isn't it? You evil bastard,' shouted Shelton when he saw two men come in to stand beside Franklyn. Then he roared, 'Get the hell out of here, all of you. Foley and my men will be coming back any time now.'

'Ah, Foley.' Franklyn sighed with a smile and then continued, 'This was his idea, but he seems to have gone missing. He was the one who killed your grandson and saved me a job. He was hoping to get his hands on that money, but he's in for a disappointment. By the way, my name isn't Franklyn, but it's a name you know well. I'm Jonathan Clarkson, the young boy you left to die in a burning house. I've got the burn marks on my body which Stephanie wouldn't have found very pretty if we had married, but there was no chance of that. Our children would have had their blood tainted with yours, you monster.'

'Just take the money and do whatever you want with me, because I'm not going to beg. Have you got Stephanie?' shouted Shelton defiantly.

'I would imagine that Ed Foley is enjoying himself with your precious granddaughter,' Franklyn mocked, then continued, 'If the rumours are true about his lusting ways you won't be giving her away at a white wedding. Look on the bright side; she might give you a great-grandson to replace Cinders Daniel. Imagine what he'd turn out to be with his mix of Shelton and Foley blood! The boy would be like the Devil's own son.'

Shelton's face flushed even more. He was shaking as he tried to stop himself from saying anything that might anger Franklyn and worsen his fate.

'I know you would never have harmed Stephanie, so why don't you do whatever you have in mind and my men can go and find Stephanie?'

'You're a smart man, Mr Shelton, and you should have guessed what I'm going to do, but it will all be clear in a few minutes.' Franklyn nodded to the men who had finished chaining Shelton to his chair and they left the study.

'Shelton, aren't you going to ask what happened to my ma, pa, brother and sister the night you had your men torch our cabin?'

'I made your pa a fair offer. He was just too stubborn for his own good, but what I did was wrong and I hope your family survived like you. It was a terrible thing to do and I admit that, but what's done is done.'

Franklyn's face reddened with anger. He raised his gun ready to smash it into Shelton's face, but he pulled back from doing so. He wanted Shelton to be fully aware of what was going to happen to him, not unconscious in his chair. He had longed for this moment, especially during the recent months when he had been in the company of this man whom he had hated so much. Today was all about retribution. He remembered hearing a saying about an eye for an eye and this was what this was about. He would have liked to have tortured this man for longer, but he must get moving. There was still Foley to think about and Steve Ross wasn't the sort to stay away from the ranch if he had reason to suspect something. Franklyn was still seething over the way Shelton had made his pathetic plea, the way he had tried to mitigate his cruel action.

'What's done, Shelton, is that you burned all of my family alive because of your greed. It was a miracle that I survived. Just a few years ago I discovered what had happened to them and that you were responsible. I heard it from the old marshal whom you bought off. I wanted to kill him there and then, but he was riddled with some painful disease and I decided to let him suffer to the end. I made a vow and today I will honour that vow.'

Shelton was more frightened than he had ever been in his life because he knew by the look in Franklyn's eyes that he was going to die very soon unless a miracle happened. His only chance was to keep Franklyn talking and hope his men would return, or even Ross. If Steve Ross turned up now he could marry Stephanie with his blessing. When he thought of Stephanie he was reminded of what Franklyn had said about Foley's lusting and he felt sick. He forced the thought from his mind and continued with what he hoped would be a delaying tactic.

'I don't understand. You've been here for months. I was

ready to welcome you into our family. Why did you wait so long?'

'My coming here was by pure chance. I thought your having the name Shelton was just a coincidence. I had heard that Conrad Shelton had died in a railroad accident and I thought that was you. I only recently discovered that it was your son who shared the same name, but that wasn't what made me realize that you were the evil monster whom I hated so much. I discovered that quite by accident when I was doing some legal work for you and I came across some old documents. I got to like Stephanie. I would probably have married her if I hadn't have found out what I did and I decided to bide my time. I just wanted revenge, not money. Then, when the kidnap notes started to arrive, I thought: why not? I have sort of stolen Foley's idea. I guess Foley just wanted to spook you by mentioning the name Clarkson in the note that I saw when I went through your papers. It's a pity Foley isn't here now, but I'll take care of him later.'

The study door was flung against the wall as the two men staggered in, each carrying a large bale of hay.

Shelton face went pale as he realized that his worst fears were about to come true.

'You can't do this. I just wanted to frighten your pa when I ordered that fire, but this is cold-blooded murder. No man deserves to die like this. I am begging you now. Just take the money and I promise that I won't send anyone after you, or involve the law. I killed the Brock brothers. You can tell Ross if I don't keep my word. I'm begging you.'

Franklyn was unmoved by the latest pleas for mercy and

just smiled again. 'Don't worry, you won't be alone. I've got a little surprise for you.'

'You won't get away with this,' Shelton said in final desperation.

'Ah, but I will. I'll come back later and put on my most sorrowful face. I'll stay around for the funerals to pay my last respects, then I'll disappear with all that money.'

Franklyn nodded to the men and they left the study to carry out some action that had clearly been worked out previously. Then he moved his face to within a few inches of Shelton's and said, 'I just want to see your face for a few more minutes, then I will wait outside until I have heard screaming. Goodbye, Mr Shelton. You will soon be on your way to hell.'

TWENTY-TWO

Ross headed out of town thinking that his previous problems about his future now seemed insignificant. At least one problem had been solved. He could forget about having a future with Stephanie Shelton. What would she think of the man who arrested her grandfather to face a certain hanging? He didn't know why Mickey Brock hadn't just killed Shelton except that maybe he wanted him to face the agony and humiliation of a trial before they put a noose around Shelton's neck.

Ross urged his horse on faster when he saw the sign that pointed to the Shelton ranch. There was no easy way to do this, but now he was thinking that he'd been foolish to come alone because Shelton probably wouldn't come quietly and he had a small army of men. When he heard the volley of shots he thought that his worst fears had come true. He pulled on the reins and waited, because the shots had not been fired in his direction. He steered his horse towards the small wooded area from where the shots had appeared to have come. He didn't know what he would discover, but he certainly never would have guessed it. Two men were lying on the ground, clearly dead and a third man was about to mount his horse.

'Mark, what's happened here?' Ross called out.

Mark Franklyn's body jolted with shock and he swung round to face the caller.

'Steve. Trust the law to arrive too late,' joked Franklyn, but he looked serious when he continued, 'These two robbed Mr Shelton and I gave chase. The money's all here. I'm going to take it into town and deposit it in the bank. If you're heading to the ranch then tell Mr Shelton that the money's safe. Perhaps he'll send some of his men out to pick up these two. Do you know them?'

Ross gave the men another look. Both of them were on their backs. One had his eyes closed and the other was staring skywards.

'I've never seen them before, so they must have been out-of-town boys. You did well, buddy. I have never seen you packing a gun before.'

Franklyn ignored the comment about his gun and said, 'When I told Stephanie about me and Robyn she was pleased just like I expected her to be. She told me that she wanted you and her to get back together again. I hope it works out for you two and that old man Shelton will come round to liking you. By the way, Stephanie has gone to stay with a friend for a few days. I'll be leaving town before she gets back, but perhaps we could have a beer or two before I leave. Anyway, I'd better get this money to a safe place.'

'Things might be about to change between me and Stephanie, but you'll hear all about it soon enough,' said Ross with some regret in his voice.

Ross turned his horse to head out of the woods, but he

drew his pistol and swung round, to see Franklyn had drawn his own six-shooter. The silence of the woods was filled with gunfire again. Franklyn fell to the ground and now there were two men with their eyes staring skywards. One of them had a bullet hole between his eyes. Lon Vickery would have been proud of Ross.

Ross dismounted to retrieve the saddle-bags of money, then headed out of the woods to continue with the unpleasant task of arresting Shelton. He was wondering why Shelton had been keeping the money in the house and figured that Franklyn had just told him a pack of lies.

Ross was still a short distance from the Shelton house when his nostrils caught the whiff of smoke. As he got closer to the house he saw flames coming out of the open front door. The place was usually a hive of activity with cowboys coming and going, but now it was deserted. His thoughts turned to the recent fire at the sheltering cabin. He spurred his horse on for the final gallop up to the entrance and dismounted before his horse had come to a stop. Entrance through the front door was impossible, but he was drawn to it by the sound of a woman's terrified screams. Ross decided it must be one of the domestic helpers. It took him three attempts before he smashed his way through the small side window close to the front door. He didn't wait to clear all the glass before he climbed through and the broken shards of glass ripped into his shirt, causing him to bleed in a number of places. There were small fires blazing in different parts of the large hall, but he could see that the fire must have started in Shelton's study. That was where the terrified cries for help were coming from. The flames formed around the top half of the study door, rising towards the ceiling. Ross was able to crawl along the ground and was soon inside the blazing room, which was filled with thick smoke. He felt his way towards the screams and dragged the chair holding the terrified woman towards the door. He decided against trying to free her, then he braced himself before he dragged the chair through the flame filled doorway and out into hall, while shielding the woman.

Ross cried out as he felt the pain from his burnt skin. He rolled on to the floor to extinguish his burning clothes while coughing from the effects of the smoke. He got to his feet and patted the stubborn flames on his trousers and shirt until they had all gone out, then he undid the chains holding the woman to the chair. The woman was still crying in between coughing and he tried to console her by telling her that she was safe.

'You got to save my grandfather,' she pleaded.

'Stephanie!' Ross cried out in surprise as he looked at her blackened face.

'Steve, my grandfather's in there, please save him. There's a man lying on the floor. I don't know who he is and I think he's already dead.'

'I will, but I need to get you outside first,' promised Ross, even though he was unsure whether he would be able to return to the blazing study.

Ross knocked the loose glass from the broken window with the butt of his pistol. When he'd finished he climbed through, then guided Stephanie out. She was still sobbing as he carried her to safety some distance from the house. He told her to stay where he had rested her on the grass.

'I'll get him out, I promise,' Ross said before he kissed

her smoke-marked, tear-stained face. He hurried towards the house and climbed through the window. The flames around the study door had dropped and he was able to rush through without crawling on the floor. The smoke inside the room had mostly cleared and he could see the back of Shelton's burnt chair.

'Shelton,' he called out as he approached the high-backed chair, but there was no answer. He turned the chair around and saw the reason for the silence. All of the flesh had been burned from Conrad Shelton's face and many other parts of his body. Ross found a spot on the chair that was cool enough to touch and pulled it towards the door. He looked around the still blazing hall and hurried to a window at the far end. He pulled down the heavy curtains, which he intended to use to cover Shelton's remains.

He was dragging the burnt-out chair through the front door when he heard Stephanie call out to him and then repeat herself.

'You've saved him,' she cried out. There was relief in her voice. Ross turned and hurried to meet her, to stop her from getting closer.

'I'm sorry, Stephanie, but your grandpa is dead. You'd best remember him as he was.'

He hugged her as she sobbed uncontrollably into his shoulder. He had never felt so helpless in all his life. He led her back to safety and went back to move Shelton's remains away from the house and out of Stephanie's sight before he returned to sit with her. Within a few minutes they were forced to move even further back as the heat from the house grew more intense. They settled near the spot to where Ross's horse had retreated. Ross was confident that the fire wouldn't reach the stables, but he decided not to take a chance. He released all the horses to run wild.

Ross sat beside Stephanie and held her hand as she recounted what her grandfather had said after Franklyn left them to die.

'Grandfather told me that he hadn't always been a good man, but he didn't deserve to die like he did.'

Ross lied when she asked him why he had called at the ranch. There seemed no point and she'd suffered enough without adding to her troubles by telling her that the grandfather she had adored had been responsible for the horrible death of the two innocent Brock brothers. He told her about his meeting with Franklyn, but she didn't rejoice at the deaths of the three men who had tried to kill her. He figured she would be in a state of shock for quite some time, and she would have to face the prospect of burying not just the remains of Conrad Shelton, but of her brother Daniel, whom he hadn't mentioned yet.

The once magnificent house was still ablaze by the time that some of the cowhands started drifting back, assuming that the reason for their being sent away had been dealt with. Stephanie had a close friend on the next ranch and it was decided that she would stay with her. Ross organized some of the men to get two wagons to take the five bodies back to the undertaker's in town, making sure that one of them would be used to take Shelton's body on its own. At least he was able to keep one promise that he had made to Stephanie.

TWENTY-THREE

The double funeral of Conrad and Daniel Shelton wasn't the lavish occasion that some folks would have expected. Ross had recovered the bodies of Daniel and Ed Foley and Abraham Tweedie had skilfully reunited Daniel's severed head with its body. Ross had made sure that Stephanie didn't know what had happened to her brother, or that he must have been Foley's partner in their attempt to extract money from Conrad Shelton by faking Daniel's kidnapping. The coffins had been laid side by side on a carriage that was pulled by the two identical black stallions that Conrad Shelton had bought for Stephanie and Daniel for their eighteenth birthday. Ross had never been aware that Daniel's horse existed and he had feared for Stephanie's safety when Mickey Brock and pulled it up outside the marshal's office.

Stephanie had discouraged the town council's plans to pay tribute to one whom they called a great man, saying that she just wanted a quiet affair. The only invited mourners were a few staff, Doc Hannington and Ross. The

138

service at the graveside was cut short when the dark clouds that had formed earlier released a downpour of rain that might signal the end of the drought if it continued.

Ross had stood on his own while Stephanie personally thanked those who attended. While he waited his attention was drawn to a man on horseback some distance away. When he saw Ross looking in his direction he waved, then rode off. Ross hoped that Mickey Brock was a man of his word. Brock had told Ross that Daniel Shelton had left Foley's hunting knife behind when he had fled from the clearing where he had been about to hack off Mickey's head. Brock had used that knife on Aitkin and he hoped that by battering Aitkin's face and burying the head if ever it was found it would appear that he, Mickey, was dead and no one would come looking for him. Then on the morning when he gave himself up he had seen Foley and Daniel Shelton near the scene of the hanging. He had shot them with Aitkin's gun. He had used Foley's own hunting-knife, and the one that had been used on his brothers, to hack off the heads of Foley and Daniel Shelton.

After the funerals most of the boys from the Shelton ranch made their way to the saloon and were soon discussing what was going to happen to them. They had heard the news about Ed Foley's death and some of those who had helped hang the Brock brothers wondered if they would be next now that they had heard that Mickey Brock had escaped!

Ross had wanted those who had been involved in the hangings to face a jury, but he had no way of proving who had been there on that cruel day.

Saul Bromley, one of the Shelton ranch hands, had told

his buddies before they went to the saloon after the funeral, that he would join them later because he needed to call in at Monckton's store first. When he did he was in for a disappointment. Norman Monckton told young Saul Bromley that the ring he had ordered for his sweetheart still hadn't arrived, Then he asked whether the funeral had gone off all right.

'I suppose it did, given everything that's happened,' Bromley replied, still thinking about the ring. 'It's getting to be a regular thing these days, but Abraham Tweedie will be pleased with all the business and we'll back again tomorrow.'

'You mean Ed Foley's funeral?' Monckton enquired.

'Ed wasn't very popular with some of the men. I hear that even his wife won't be going, but some of us will be there. Mary Foley seems to be more interested in wanting to find out where Jim Tully has disappeared to than about Ed's death.'

Monckton expressed his surprise that Martha Aitkin hadn't been at the Shelton funeral. Bromley offered an explanation when he replied.

'It must have all been too much for her coming after Tim's death. She probably worried what was going to happen to her now that the big house has gone. The strange thing was that when one of the boys went around last night to tell her what had happened and that we had just found out that Ed Foley was dead as well, Martha actually smiled. She seemed pleased by the news and when we called to take her to the funeral this morning she told us she wasn't going and was preparing to leave.'

*

140

Martha Aitkin had waited until mid-afternoon, just after the cowhands had returned from the Shelton funerals, before she arranged her lift into town to catch the evening stagecoach, but first she had to call in at Norman Monckton's store.

'I don't normally buy second-hand pistols, Martha,' said Norman Monckton when she placed it on the counter and asked if she could have her money back. When he saw the dejected look on her face as she explained that she was hoping to catch the stagecoach to go and live with her sister in Cheney Falls he said he would make an exception in her case.

Monckton handed her the money and jokingly asked her whether she had changed her mind about robbing the bank?

'If I told you the real reason why I bought that pistol, Mr Monckton, I don't expect you'd believe me, but I had no need in the end because the Good Lord did the job for me. Goodbye, Mr Monckton. I hope you and the town prosper now that the evil has been removed.'

Norman Monckton bade her farewell and wished her luck. He had never considered that Martha had been much of a believer in religious matters and he wondered what she had been referring to. He guessed he would never really know, except it must have something to do with the Sheltons.

Monckton's next caller was a man who gave him the creeps even though he had known him for many years. It was Abraham Tweedie. He looked troubled and he was carrying a small card.

'You looked tired, Abraham. I expect these sad times

141

mean you are kept busy.'

Abraham didn't comment on Monckton's observations and asked him if he would display in his shop the card he was holding. He told Monckton that he had put a larger notice on the front of the funeral parlour. The notice had been written with a shaky hand, but it was still plain enough to see. It read: *Assistant Urgently Required.*

Monckton readily agreed after he had read the notice. Then he said, 'I heard that Luke Mason had given up being your assistant. I was surprised because he was in here just a few weeks ago telling me how much he enjoyed the work. Did you two have a falling-out?'

'The boy was a hard worker and I'm sorry that he is no longer in my employ,' replied Tweedie in a formal tone, then added, 'Let's just say that he didn't think it was something he would like to spend the rest of his life doing. My profession is more of a vocation. Anyway, I am probably going to retire soon, especially if I am not able to hire an assistant.'

Abraham had been thinking a lot lately that perhaps it was time to give up his business. He was sad that he wouldn't have a son to pass it on to, but women had never warmed to him. He wondered whether it was because he hadn't been blessed with good looks. The long nose that seemed to have sprouted with his height when he'd been fifteen years old had grown even longer, and his face had become gaunt now that he was sixty-eight years old. Business had never been brisker thanks to the recent bout of gruesome deaths, but it wasn't all good news. That boy Mason had seemed so promising when he started, eager to learn and now he was gone. The sight of Conrad Shelton's charred remains and the smell of burnt flesh had been bad enough, and then, when the marshal had brought those two heads along, Mason had puked and walked out. Luke Mason's ma had called around to say that he wouldn't be coming back.

Now there were more problems because the man who made his coffins had run out of timber and he didn't know whether he would be able to make one for Ed Foley because he'd used the last wood to make the Shelton coffins. He'd always worried about leaving it too late to leave Craigy Plains before he died. Tweedie was thinking that that day might not be too far away, unless he got to live as long as his pa who'd died on his eighty-second birthday. The prospect of being buried amongst those he had been the last person to gaze upon before the coffin was sealed was something that caused him sleepless nights.

Tweedie had always treated the people he buried with respect and dignity, regardless of how they had conducted their lives and it wasn't for him to judge them.

He had been a good friend of the town's first preacher, Reverend Thomas Lucas Stanforth. Doc Hannington had been away when someone had come running into Tweedie's funeral parlour and said the preacher had collapsed in church while practising his sermon for the next Sunday. Tweedie was no medical man, but he was better suited to declaring a man dead than any other man in town, so that was what he did when he saw his ashen-faced friend lying beside his pulpit. The preacher was approaching his seventy-second birthday and had never been in the best of health, but Tweedie was still shocked that he had lost his best friend. Reverend Stanforth had been laid to rest in the town cemetery for almost three years and hardly a day went by when Tweedie didn't recall that moment when he'd prepared to place the lid on the preacher's coffin. At the time he had convinced himself that he was overtired, that he had imagined his friend's eyes opening and displaying a look of terror and that when he had touched his face it must have been his imagination that it felt warm. He didn't know why he had hurriedly closed the lid instead of checking properly that his friend really was dead and now he would spend the rest of his days trying to convince himself that he hadn't buried a man alive. He couldn't face the prospect of being buried next to him.

Monckton was a bit surprised at the news about Abraham thinking of retiring, but told him that he had earned it and it would give him more time to spend on his hobby, which was taxidermy. Tweedie had reached the doorway when Monckton shouted after him that he hoped any new undertaker would give both of them a good burial when the time came.

Tweedie had heard the remark, but he was not amused.

TWENTY-FOUR

During the week following the Shelton funerals Ross wanted to go and see Stephanie, but he didn't think it was right. He was certain that her emotions must be all haywire. He would bide his time, hoping that the feelings she had shown to him would still be there. In the meantime he had to get used to being the town marshal now that Ed Foley wouldn't be coming back.

The rain, which had started on the day of Conrad Shelton's funeral, had continued for several days. Old Matt Wethered, who considered himself something of a weather forecaster, mainly because he had studied it since he was teased as a boy about his name, said that there was much more to come. So, maybe the farmers and ranchers would soon be celebrating.

The town council had timidly told Ross that John Healey, who ran the Elm House saloon had complained that his takings were down because Ross was being too heavy-handed with high-spirited cowboys and some were staying away. Ross told them that he would ease off a little, but he had no intention of letting off anyone who misused

145

a six-shooter and endangered innocent folks.

Ross had tried to fathom the events surrounding the tragic deaths. Stephanie had told him that Mark Franklyn had persuaded her to stay in the hotel in town. He said that it had been her grandfather's idea, to keep her safe. Ross realized that it must have been Stephanie he had seen going into the hotel and Franklyn had been lying when he'd told Ross it was a woman from Franklyn's past. On the day that she nearly died in the fire Franklyn had said earlier that it was safe for her to go home. On the way to the house the evil man had even said that he still wanted to marry her. Ross told Stephanie that it was a mystery why her brother was with Foley when they were killed by Mickey Brock, but that was only to spare her feelings. Ross didn't have any doubt that Foley and Daniel must have been working together. He wished that he could lay his hands on the man who had terrified Stephanie and pretended to have kidnapped Daniel. It was possible that Daniel had been the one to start the fire in the cabin to fake his own death and maybe Stephanie's tormentor had just been used by Foley and he was the one who had perished in the fire. Ross doubted if he would ever discover whether Franklyn was working with Foley and Daniel, but had planned all along to take his revenge on the Shelton family.

Exactly two weeks after the Shelton funerals Ross had a surprise visitor to the marshal's office. It was Stephanie Shelton, and Hank Lewis made some excuse for leaving so that they could be on their own. Ross was pleased to see that she was looking better, although her eyes were still showing signs of her grieving. He let her talk, hoping that it would help. She didn't make any excuses for her evil grandfather and her brother, Daniel, whom she now believed must have been involved. She just felt sorrow for the misery that people had suffered. She didn't mention Mark Franklyn, whose hatred had nearly been the cause of her own death.

When she said she felt guilty about not standing up to her grandfather because if she had they would have been happy together, Ross interrupted.

'We still can be. I know we never stopped loving each other even though I thought you had when I heard talk of you marrying Franklyn.'

'I never would have married him,' Stephanie replied quietly.

'I know, but now we can be together like we'd talked about before. . . .' Ross stopped himself from mentioning her grandfather again.

'That's what I hoped you'd say, but I could never live here after all that's happened. I'm leaving town tomorrow and going to stay with my mother's family in Bay Creek.'

Ross looked disappointed when he said, 'So, you've come to say goodbye?'

'It won't be if you come with me,' she said smiling.

Ross was taken aback. When he'd recovered he said that they could make a new start. They kissed and hugged and the sadness and trauma left Stephanie. She was happier than she had been for a very long time. They talked and talked about the things that they might do with their new life and they agreed that Ross would join her in a month's time after he had served notice. It would also give Stephanie the chance to prepare her relatives for the arrival of the man she planned to marry.

Hank Lewis had been chinwagging across the street. When he saw Stephanie leave he made his way back to the office. The look on Ross's face told him that the reunion had gone well, but he wasn't prepared for the news that Ross would be leaving.

'I would say that you will be in for a pay rise when you become marshal,' said Ross after he told Hank that he would be leaving in a month.

'The money would be handy, but I'm not ready to be a marshal, Steve. In fact I was thinking of applying for that vacancy as Abraham Tweedie's assistant, but Moira threatened not to let me near her if I had been touching cold corpses. So, I'll give the marshal's job a go if you think I can manage it, but it won't be for long now that we've had all that rain. I've already told Moira that I'll be going back to farming at the start of the planting season and she's mighty relieved.'

'You'll be fine, Hank, but I think you've made the right decision about going back to work on your place. If we don't get enough rain you can always join Abraham. I'll ask Abraham to keep the position open if you like.'

Hank replied, 'Don't you dare, I was only joking about Abraham's job.' They both laughed.

Ross wasn't much good at letter-writing, but he had sent Stephanie two letters by the time he was packing to catch the train the next day which would take him to her and the beginning of a new life. The town council had expressed some reservation about appointing Hank in his

148

place, but accepted that he had done well in a short time and approved his appointment.

When Ross had finished clearing out his desk he took a final look around the office. Memories of Marshal Waters flashed before him. They were mostly good memories. He didn't dwell on those of Mickey Brock's visit and the gruesome contents of the blankets. He was feeling good as he crossed the street to the Elm House and his meeting with Hank and a farewell beer or two before he said his goodbyes to people like Doc Hannington. The sound of gunfire as he prepared to open the swing doors of the saloon didn't cause him any alarm. The ceiling of the saloon was full of holes caused by exuberant cowboys celebrating a win at cards, or some other happy event. What did cause him alarm was the eerie silence when he entered the saloon, just before he saw Hank Lewis lying on the floor, his shirt front reddened with his blood. Doc Hannington was making his way towards his friend, but Ross could see that Hank was beyond help. Ross was about to ask who had done it when he saw that a man standing at the bar was already reaching for his pistol. Perhaps it was Ross's anger that caused him to miss the intended target; the bullet entered the man's left eye rather than going between the eyes.

Ross holstered his gun, knelt beside the doc, then cradled his dead buddy. He blamed himself for agreeing to take Hank on and now he was thinking how he was going to break the news to his wife and her young children. Ross would be feeling even worse later when he learned that the gunman had coming looking for him and had mistaken Hank for him. It seemed that the gunman hadn't been hired by anyone, but was just trying to make a name for himself by killing the man who had shot Sloan.

Breaking the news to Moira Lewis and attending Hank's funeral a few days later was the most painful experience of Ross's life. The town council had paid for the funeral and given Moira a small sum of money, but Ross knew that it wouldn't last long. Moira had told him that she had no living kinfolk whom she could turn to, and Ross feared that she might even take her own life, such was the desperate state she was in. Ross had never been one for churchgoing and right now he was thinking that God had a funny way of looking after the good folks. If he was so almighty, why didn't he send down that damn rain when it was wanted? Then Hank Lewis would still be alive.

Ross's plans to join Stephanie were put on hold when he decided that he would stay on as marshal and help support Hank's family until things improved. So he wrote to Stephanie, explaining the situation. She seemed to understand but, as the months went by, her letters were less frequent. He wasn't entirely surprised when a letter arrived containing an ultimatum that he join her very soon, or she would consider that their relationship was over. He understood her position; she had been patient and he wrote and told her that he would join her in two months' time. She never replied. Later something happened that made him feel that perhaps it was for the best and maybe it was never meant to be.

TWENTY-FIVE

It had been four months since Hank Lewis's death when Ross eventually found a deputy who was suitable. Kirk Johansson had been recommended by a marshal from Benson County and Ross was grateful to have him on board because there had been an increase in trouble over at the Elm House saloon. Kirk Johansson was twenty-three years old and a slightly built man, with blond hair and blue eyes that he'd inherited from his ma and pa who had both hailed from Sweden. Despite not being an imposing figure, Kirk Johansson had a confident manner that seemed to dissuade most cowboys from tangling with him when he was issuing a warning to them. He had already been forced to shoot a man dead outside the saloon, so Ross had no worries on that score. Ross was going on leave in the morning and he was confident that his deputy could handle things while he was away. Ross planned to take the train to Wesley City and see what life was like in a place that was twenty or more times the size of Craigy Plains.

Dusk was approaching when the two strangers in town sat down on the bench on the sidewalk near the barber-shop.

'What did you find out, Deak?' Morrie asked.

'The old marshal who threw us out of town is dead. He was gunned down by Sloan. Remember we saw Sloan shoot those two fellers off that cattle drive when we were in . . . er . . . I forget the name of the place?'

'Yeah, I remember Sloan,' Morrie replied with a yawn.

'Sloan's dead as well,' Deak said, then added, 'and the feller who shot Sloan is the one we've come to get even with and now he's the new marshal. He actually spoke to me in the saloon, but I don't think he recognized me. His name is Ross. I nearly bumped into him when I was leaving, now he's doing his rounds of the town and should be coming back this way any time now.'

Deak couldn't see Morrie's face in the dark, but if he could he would have seen the troubled look on it.

'He wasn't even wearing a gun that night he made a mess of us just because you slapped that old hag in the saloon. He must be pretty handy with a weapon if he took out Sloan, unless he shot him in the back. We'll have to make sure he doesn't get a chance to get a shot off.'

Deak gave a snigger and said, 'Don't you worry because we ain't going face to face with him; but we're going to give him a good beating before we finish him off. Then we leave town and in a few weeks we'll be able to come and go as we please and sample some of those women that feller was telling us about.'

'What if that old bitch in the saloon recognizes us?' Morrie asked.

'I didn't tell you that bit. She left town months ago with some dude from back East who planned to marry her.'

'I know we can take this feller, Deak, but I'm wondering

152

if it's worth it just so that we can start visiting this town again? It just ain't that special.'

'This isn't just about being able to come back into town when we like. That feller made a mess of my face and we've got a score to settle.' Deak fingered his lopsided jaw – a habit he'd developed ever since he realized how ugly it made him look.

Deak had spotted someone walking towards them. 'Anyway, he's coming this way now,' he announced. 'Just slump back and pretend to be asleep.'

Ross was whistling quietly as he approached the bench and then smiled when he looked down at the two men who, he assumed, were sleeping it off after having too much liquor. He was tempted to shake them awake and tell them to move, but they weren't doing any harm, so he walked on.

Ross was in the process of turning around when the butt of Deak's gun smashed into the side of his face. Morrie's gun was delivered with equal force to the back of Ross's head and he fell off the sidewalk into the street. Ross's attackers jumped off the sidewalk, taking no chances that Ross might get to his feet, and began kicking him even though he was already unconscious. He briefly regained consciousness and groaned as they took turns in delivering vicious kicks to his face and body. Deak used one of his spurs as a weapon and stroked it across Ross's face. Deak and Morrie were gasping for breath as a result of the assault and had paused briefly when they heard the shout from across the street.

'Drop your weapons, now!' was the firm order. Both men fired off a shot in the direction of the caller, but missed him in the fading light in Main Street. The first of Deputy Karl Johansson's shots hit Deak in the throat and his second thudded into Morrie's chest. When Johansson reached the three men lying alongside each other Morrie was already dead and Deak's gurgling sound as the blood bubbled from his mouth soon stopped. It took a moment before the deputy realized that the man with horrific injuries to his face was Ross.

Johansson wasn't normally the sort to panic, but now he did, just for a moment. Then he raced off in the direction of Doc Hannington's surgery. Johansson's banging on the surgery door grew more rapid and louder until he saw a light flicker on inside. On another occasion he would normally have smiled when he saw Doc Hannington standing in the doorway, wearing a long nightshirt and holding a candle, but now he blurted out the terrible news of the attack on his buddy, Ross. The doc said it was best if Johansson got some men to carry Ross back to the surgery while he got dressed and prepared things.

Doc Hannington had seen the results of some vicious beatings in his time, the worst being caused by a glass or broken bottle being thrust into a man's face, but Ross's disfigured face was as bad as anything he'd ever witnessed.

An hour after Ross had been placed on the surgery table only the occasional weak groan indicated that he was still alive. Doc Hannington was thinking that maybe it would be kinder if Ross didn't survive, but he would do all he could to help the young man live.

It was barely daylight and the rest of the townsfolk were still asleep when Johansson tapped lightly on the doc's surgery door. It was opened by a bleary-eyed and tired-looking Doc Hannington. Johansson crept inside. He looked down at Ross and winced because the face looked worse than it had the previous night. It had ballooned in places and the blueness of the bruises was mixed with the redness of the dried blood. Johansson was relieved when he saw Ross's chest rise and fall.

'He's still hanging on then, Doc?'

The doc sighed heavily. 'He has no right to, given the damage he's suffered, but I think he's going to make it,' he replied. 'Many a man wouldn't in his state.'

The doc had left the surgery briefly the night before to formally declare dead the two men who had been shot by Johansson. One of the men had a bushy beard and he couldn't be certain that he'd seen him before, but he remembered treating the other one. If Ross survived he might have to tell him that he was the man whom he was supposed to have killed the day before he became a deputy marshal.

TWENTY-SIX

Ross stood up from his chair on the porch of his family home and stretched his arms before sitting down again next to Lon Vickery. Lon was frail now and the hair had finally turned grey. Lon's faithful dog, Boy, was by his side, but it wasn't the same dog that Ross saw that day when he visited Lon to learn how to handle a pistol. The dog was the first to hear the carriage and barked with excitement, mostly because Sam Lewis was seated up front. Sam was Hank Lewis's eldest son and was aged twelve. Ross still had regrets that he'd allowed Hank to become his deputy because he would still be alive if Ross hadn't given in to his desperate pleas for the job. Boy wagged his tail furiously when young Sam jumped from the carriage and patted him. Ross smiled as his wife got down from the carriage she had driven into town with Sam and Ross's own children. Ross smiled again as his wife approached carrying some small packages. She bent down and gave him a lingering kiss, while pushing his holster to one side. Life was peaceful in this part of Arizona now, but both men were always armed.

*

It was six years since Stephanie Ross had the lovely house built a short distance from where her father's grand house had once stood. When Stephanie had received Ross's last letter she was feeling insecure and felt that he was just playing for time. Perhaps he had grown fond of Hank's widow. Stephanie was a wealthy young woman and had planned to travel the world, but she never did. She had thought about Ross a lot during the first year after her grandfather's death and had been devastated when their plans to start a new life together didn't happen. She had regretted giving him the ultimatum and had considered going to see him in the hope that there was still a chance for them to get together. Then she feared that Ross had perhaps married Moira Lewis.

Stephanie might have spent the rest of her days wondering and regretting about Ross, had it not been for a chance meeting with someone from her past. So, she returned to face her demons and marry the man she loved.

'Stop that, you two,' Lon joked and they both laughed.

'I wish you two wouldn't still carry those guns,' Stephanie scolded them playfully.

'We're not as trusting as you, honey and perhaps it's the lawman in me. I was thinking of wearing my old badge just to show you who's in charge around here. Perhaps I will when little Steve is a bit older if he starts getting cheeky.'

Stephanie gave Ross a playful pat on the shoulder and told him that he was too soft with the children.

Ross sometimes reflected how things might have been if Marshal Waters had lived. He wondered if the old-timer would have approved what he did with Mickey Brock, who had confessed to killing Tim Aitkin, Ed Foley and Daniel Shelton. After the Shelton funerals Ross had decided that Mickey Brock had suffered enough and, in Ross's eyes, didn't deserve to hang. So, Ross had let Mickey Brock escape in return for a promise to leave the county. Ross had never seen or heard of Mickey Brock since he waved to him at the cemetery on the day the remains of Conrad Shelton were buried.

One of the saloon girls had told Ross that a drunken cowboy had been babbling on about how rich he would have been if Ed Foley hadn't messed things up. A lot of what he'd said didn't make sense, but he claimed that he was the one who took part in the fake kidnap of Daniel Shelton. Then Foley had got him to start the fire in the sheltering cabin where Foley had kept Jim Tully prisoner. Foley had an old score to settle with Tully because he had been messing about with his wife. The man had escaped over the bridge just before Conrad Shelton arrived at the cabin. What happened to Tully had played on his mind ever since. The man had left the girl and started trouble at the card-table when he tried to cheat and ended up dead after he was shot in the throat.

Ross's agonizing over whether he'd done the right thing in letting Brock go free was tempered when he later made a shocking discovery. On the night he was attacked he had seen a man in the saloon who he had thought looked familiar, but it couldn't have been the man he was thinking about because he was dead and Ross was supposed to have killed him. When he recovered from his severe beating he'd mentioned it to Doc Hannington and the old doc confessed that Marshal Waters had asked him to support his lie so that he could 'blackmail' Ross into becoming a lawman. So Ross realized that he wasn't the only lawman who had bent the law. He quietly cursed the old marshal, but it had brought a smile to his face and he discovered later that old Lon also knew about the marshal's ruse to get him to become a deputy. He would also reflect that had he not been a lawman when Franklyn carried out his revenge attack, then his beautiful Stephanie would have met with the same fate has her evil grandfather.

Stephanie shouted to the children, who were playing with the dog, to come inside while she prepared some food for them all. When Ross heard Lon's gentle snoring he got up and whispered to Stephanie that he was going for a ride. She was on the verge of telling him to be careful, but stopped herself because she knew it would make him cross.

'I hope you've got something nice in mind for grub,' he said before he kissed her. He stepped down off the veranda and untied the reins of his horse which were secured to the hitch rail.

She watched him ride off on the sorrel that she had bought him for his last birthday and gave a sigh. Life was good for Stephanie and filled with happiness. It might have all been so different if fate had not delivered another cruel blow when Ross was blinded when he was attacked from behind by those men. Kirk Johansson was now the marshal and paid regular visits to chinwag with Ross. Moira Lewis was living in the cabin that was once occupied by Martha Aitkin. She remarried three years after the loss of her Hank and she and her children were happy again.

Stephanie had blotted out the memory of her grandfather and brother and never visited the cemetery and the Shelton graves where they were buried.

If Stephanie ever decided to visit the graves of her family members she would pass by the grave of Abraham Tweedie, who collapsed and died while trying to carry an empty coffin into his funeral parlour. The town council thought that it would be fitting if the respected undertaker's final resting-place should be in the grave next to his old friend Thomas Lucas Stanforth, the town's first preacher!

A doctor back East said that it was possible that Ross might regain his sight one day, but Stephanie and Ross knew that it would take a miracle. They considered that they already had two miracles called Steve and Beth. Life was good for them all.